A Woman's Glimpse
into her Fantasies

Tantalizing Desires

Lori A Heslegrave

 **FriesenPress**

Suite 300 - 990 Fort St
Victoria, BC, V8V 3K2
Canada

www.friesenpress.com

Copyright © 2021 by Lori A Heslegrave
First Edition — 2021

All rights reserved.

No part of this publication may be reproduced in any form, or by any means, electronic or mechanical, including photocopying, recording, or any information browsing, storage, or retrieval system, without permission in writing from FriesenPress.

ISBN
978-1-03-911354-1 (Hardcover)
978-1-03-911353-4 (Paperback)
978-1-03-911355-8 (eBook)

1. FICTION, EROTICA

Distributed to the trade by The Ingram Book Company

Dedication

To my children, Ainsley and Shaymus, who stood by me and supported me as I wrote this book, which I know they will never read.

To Vanessa, my soundboard, who would listen as I kicked ideas around, who gave me feedback to work with, and who drank my margaritas.

To William, my inspiration, the man I fell in love with, who encouraged me to write this book. Though we were physically apart, you were always close in my heart as I sat and wrote these stories.

To my editors, my publisher, my designers, and everyone else at Friesen Press who made my dream a reality, I thank you all.

Finally, to Isolde, Caroline, and Gary, who supported me through this journey.

I thank you.

Introduction

There is romance, there is fantasy, and there is sex. There is what the world used to think of as erotica, and what today we see as modern romance.

In the mid-1930s, Pietro Ramirez Sr. published a book titled, *How to make love*. This was an illustrated compendium of ways to gain someone's love, with the intention of one day marrying them.

By the 1940s, people were talking more about sex in scientific terms, which were also defined in a marital context. Sex, we were told, could only bring you happiness if you were married.

The 1950s brought about a new way of looking at sex and dating. The young of the 1950s viewed dating as a possible path into marriage, but after the war, "going Steady" just meant that you were dating with no prelude to marriage. Sex was allowed.

The ideas of romance, sex, and fantasy have taken on many other definitions as the years have gone on. With the identification of many new genders, the society in which we live may perceive these three ideas as being based on culture or social norms.

But the readers of romance have seen a transformation of how romance is now perceived. Romance writing today touches on this fact of life.

Romance, sex, and fantasy—they are all true facts of life. We may daydream about them each day, or we may experience them at times.

I have written these short stories based on ideas that I have fantasized about or that were given to me by other romantic thinkers.

The stories in this collection will discuss each of these ideas. Accordingly, they are divided into two sections: Fantasy and Love. Sex permeates both sections, but you will find that the flavors of these stories changes, as do our heroes' goals, hopes, and actions.

Readers, take a seat and read with an open mind, knowing that fantasies can become a reality.

Lori A Heslegrave

Fantasy

The Paperboy	5
The Stepmom	15
The Swingers	21
The Homecoming	31

The aperboy

Ruby was certain that he would walk by her house again, as he always did on Wednesdays and Fridays at four p.m. She would say to herself, "One day, I will teach that boy."

He crossed the cul-de-sac between Mr. Bains's and Ms. Harper's houses. She could see him heading her way, dressed in his torn blue jeans and his retro eighties t-shirt, pulling his wagon of newspapers.

How many of those damn t-shirts does he have? she asked herself.

His route was simple: two culs-de-sac and one apartment building. Not too bad, seeing as it paid him $150 a month, and even more during the spring festival season.

"Really, why is it that every year at the same time, people need to be reminded of the stupid spring festival?" he said to his parents.

"Aw don't complain my son. The spring festival and all its advertising gives you an extra $50. That brings you $50 closer to getting that car you want so badly," said his dad.

Ruby stepped off her porch and walked to the mailbox at the end of the driveway. "Hello Paperboy."

Ruby looked so elegant in her pencil blue skirt and white floral blouse. He could see the outline of her bra under her blouse, and when she leaned forward to grab the paper, he could see her breast poking out of the top of her bra.

"I do have a name, you know."

"Yeah I know," she said as she grabbed the paper and walked away. "Oh, Paperboy? When you're old enough to date and have a car, I will let you touch them."

He stood there; cheeks as red as his wagon. He watched her walk up the walkway into her house. "Two more years," he said. "Just two more and the car is mine."

He had been delivering the newspaper since he was twelve. Every delivery day, he would think about seeing Ruby. Ruby was seven years older than him, but this did not bother him. He would tell his friends that she would be his first. He often tried to fantasize about what it would be like, but all he knew was what he saw on those videos his dad had hidden in the attic, and he knew enough to know that they were not what it was going to be like. By the time he was eighteen, he had saved more than enough to buy himself a car, and he still had his paper route. Walking toward Ruby house on Tuesday, he saw her coming down the walkway to the mailbox, as she had been doing since he started his route six years earlier. He admired her, as he did every week. He took in her plump breasts, her swivelling hips, and her seductive smile. But this time it was different. This time, he knew that she would soon be his.

"Hi Ruby, guess what I finally got?"

"Herpes," she said with a giggle.

"A new car. So, you owe me."

"What the hell do I owe you, Paperboy?"

"Well, you said that when I was old enough and have a car, I could finally touch your breast. Well, I am eighteen now, and I have a car. So, I will pick you up Friday at 8:00."

Then he walked away, head held high. Ruby stood in shock, knowing very well that she did make him that promise some years ago. She knew the next few days were going to be hard on her, as she was certain that she would need to teach him a few things. The question was, where to start?

Ruby was standing by the mailbox waiting for him in her favourite green wraparound dress, which outlined her curves. Her long curls decorated her neck like a piece of jewelry.

"Hop in," he said.

"Aren't you going to open the door for me?"

He got out of the car, walked over to her side, and opened the door for her. Her body brushed his as she got into the car, sending a shiver down his body and a tingle in his groin. "There you go, Milady," as he bowed before closing the car door. Ruby giggled.

They drove in silence to the beach. When they arrived, he got out of the car, grabbing a basket from the back seat. As he started walking to the beach, he stopped and looked at her, asking, "Are you coming?"

They walked down the beach, to an area that housed a little semicircular tent that had a net for a roof and a bamboo sheet for a floor. He sat the basket down, then he grabbed her hand and told her to sit and relax.

"Want a drink?" he asked her as he opened the basket.

"Sure, what have you to offer?"

"Beer, wine or pop, and if you want pot, I got that too."

"I'll take the wine, and yes to the pot!"

They sat there, drinking, smoking, and listening to the waves hit the shore. He spoke. "So, Ruby, I brought you here to collect what you owe me."

Ruby smiled at him, saying, "Let's start with a kiss." He bent over and kissed her. She was surprised that he could kiss. He proceeded to grab her breast. Ruby grabbed his hand and said, "Not like that. Here, let me show you how." She guided his hands where she wanted them and brought his mouth to her neck. "First, you need to give me butterfly kisses as you hold one breast in your hand, like this." She placed his hand on her breast and she could feel his heat through her dress. "Now, slowly and softly tease my breast until you feel my nipple become erect."

"Like this?" he asked.

"Yes, just like that."

As he was rubbing her breast, her dress became looser, exposing her beige bra. He could see the outline of her nipple through the thin fabric. "Hmmm," she moaned. "That's good."

He was becoming aroused as he continued to play with her breast. "Now, pull my bra away from my breast and, using your fingertips, play with my nipple."

He followed her direction and could feel her nipple responding to his touch. He was becoming hard, and his cock was beginning to feel uncomfortable in his pants. He started to squirm, trying to find a position that did not irritate his cock. Ruby noticed him fidgeting about and pulled back, asking him, "What is wrong?" Then, she noticed the full erection hiding in his pants. Smiling at him, she proceeded to unzip his jeans and retrieve his cock. Holding it in her hands, he started to moan, and she knew he would come soon.

"Relax, take a deep breath," she moved away from him and stood up. "Look at me," she said in a sexy demanding voice. As he looked up at her, she proceeded to remove her dress and unfasten her bra. Standing there in her G-string, she started to play with her erect nipples. She licked her fingertips and rubbed them against her nipples as he watched and eventually ejaculated over himself.

The drive home was quiet. Arriving at her house, Ruby looked at him and said, "I will be alone for the weekend. Come by tomorrow around noon, and I will make you lunch and teach you some more." She got out of the car. Then, before leaving, she leaned into the passenger side window and said, "Here, a little reminder of tonight," and she threw him her bra.

On his drive home, all he could remember was her erect nipples and how he wanted to suck on them so badly. He knew that he would have that opportunity soon.

He could not sleep that night, knowing that tomorrow he would finally make love to the woman he had always wanted. He tossed and turned, unable to find a comfortable position. His cock was growing as he thought about her. He started to play with himself before he was interrupted by a clanking sound on his bedroom window. Getting up to look out the window, he could see a faint shadow under the hibiscus tree.

"Who's there?" he called out in a low voice.

"It's me, Ruby. Can I come in?"

He could not believe his ears when he heard her voice. "Yeah, hold on. I am coming down."

He raced out of his room to the back door to let in. "What the hell are you doing here?" he asked her.

"What do you think?" She stepped closer to him and kissed him. He could not contain himself and pulled her closer to him. His erect penis was throbbing against her groin. "Come on," he said, "let us go upstairs."

"Wait, are your parents' home? They may catch us."

He looked at her and smiled. "No, they are out of country for another six weeks."

They proceeded to the staircase when she noticed an array of pictures hanging on the wall. "Are they your parents? Do you know who he is?"

He stood looking at her laughing. "Yes, I am aware of who my dad is. Does it bother you?"

She continued looking at the photos on the wall before saying, "No, not at all."

They entered his room at the far end of the hallway. "My God," said Ruby. "You need a bloody map to find your way around this place." He opened the door to his room and led her in. Ruby stood in the centre of the room looking around admiring the décor. "Wow!" she said before turning to him.

Tantalizing Desires

Ruby walked closer to him, asking if he was ready for the next lesson. Looking down at his pajama bottoms, she could see him standing at attention. "Oh, you are ready."

Ruby noticed a wet spot on his pajama bottoms and said, "*Oh, looks like you have a leak. Let me fix that for you.*" She proceeded to bend down, pulling the pajama bottoms as she descended. Taking his hard, wet cock in her hands, she slowly started to tease the tip. He moaned and held her head closer. Her tongue ran up and down his shaft as she teased his balls with her hands.

"That's it, babe, enjoy," said Ruby between licking and sucking his cock. He knew he could no longer contain himself, and he blew his load deep into her mouth. Ruby continued licking his shaft. "There we go, all clean," she said. He stood there with a smile on his face, realizing he wanted to learn more.

"Now let me teach you how to go down on me," Ruby said as she undressed and lay herself on his bed. She spread her legs for him to see her full beauty.

"Now, Paperboy, look. You see this?" She pointed to her throbbing clit. "I want you to lick it and suck it like an ice cream cone."

He climbed on to the bed and started to tease her clit with the tip of his tongue. He could feel her body reacting, and he knew he was doing it right.

"Now, suck on it, Paperboy. Take it between your lips and suck hard." He followed her directions as she raised her body off the bed, moaning.

"That's it, now give me your hand." He gave her his hand. She guided it to her wet vagina, pushing his finger inside of her. Her body was responding as he placed another finger inside of her, feeling her wetness. "You're a quick learner, Paperboy."

He could feel her spasm from the inside out, her body rising as he pushed his fingers deeper and harder into her. He wanted more of her. He wanted to feel her on his hard cock. He removed his fingers and guided himself up to her face, where he could look into her green eyes. Slowly, Ruby guided his cock inside of her, pushing her body upward, taking all of him. He moaned in pleasure.

Ruby whispered into his ear, "Take your time. Take your time."

He listened to her words and thrust himself deeper and deeper into her, slowly feeling her body respond to his every move. "That's it. Harder, Paperboy, harder!"

He could not contain himself and pushed himself deeper and harder until she came. He could feel her hot liquid covering his penis. He continued thrusting his hard cock into her until he came.

Ruby rolled him over and sat on top of him. "Not too shabby, Paperboy. Not to shabby at all for your first time." She started to kiss his chest, then his neck, while one hand remained behind her playing with his cock. As she kissed his lips, she said, "Care to learn more?"

He smiled and replied with a kiss. Ruby raised her body till her wet pussy reached his face. She did not need to tell him anything, as he was a quick learner. He sucked on her swollen clit and teased her pussy with his tongue, sucking and licking as she rode his face, squirting as she came. He was shocked, as he did not know what this meant.

"What did you just do?" he asked.

Ruby giggled saying, "I squirted." He smiled and reminded himself to look up "squirting" after she left.

I learned a lot from Ruby. Since my many encounters with her, I have craved the sensation of pleasuring women. Ruby taught me that a woman's needs go beyond simple intercourse. She needs her body to be indulged with attention to her every move. She needs the sweet taste of her nectar to be savoured when she is aroused and ready to come. You need to listen to her body talking to you as it guides you onto a path of arousal with her. To come alone is enjoyment, but to come together is the pure gratification of the senses.

The Stepmom

I was twenty at the time; it was the nineties, where style was about putting on something that was fun and easy. It was Saturday night. I had been out clubbing the night before with my friends, as we did every Friday and Saturday. I knew that Sunday would be spent catching up on schoolwork that was due by Tuesday.

This Saturday night, we had all been drinking more than we were accustomed to. My friends dared me to pick up this older woman. We saw her sitting at the bar almost every weekend. How could I turn down such a challenge?

Walking up to the bar, I ordered myself a drink and started to talk to her. She had this aura about her that seemed to pull me in. I wanted to know more about her—who she was, what she did, and most of all, could I have sex with her? She had the most beautiful blonde hair, and it bounced on her shoulders every time she laughed. She had generous breasts, and her nipples peaked through the light blue fabric of her spaghetti strap dress. Her legs were crossed, which exposed her thigh. I could only imagine that she was not wearing anything under that dress.

I asked her to dance. When we reached the dance floor, she held her arms out by her side and twirled until she fell into my arms. Holding her close, I could smell her sweet scent.

"What are we going to do after we dance?" I asked her.

She replied, "I am taking you home so you can fuck my brains out." Then she kissed me passionately. "I am Aurora, but my friends call me Dawn."

I could not believe what she had just said. So, I grabbed her hand and said, "Let's go now." It was about an hour before closing time, and she agreed.

We got our stuff together, and I said goodbye to my buddies, who were shocked that I was walking out with the hottest cougar in the bar. We grabbed a cab outside, and off we went.

We could not keep our hands off each other on the ride to her house. She then decided that I needed a blow job in the taxi. "No, not here." I said.

She winked and went down on me. The cab driver kept turning around to catch a glimpse. I had to tell him to keep his eyes on the road, and that I would give him a good tip when we got to our destination. The cab pulled up in front of a beautiful house, just as she finished draining me. She paid the cabbie his fare, and I gave him a $20 tip as I rushed out of the back seat, somewhat embarrassed.

I still could not believe that this was happening. Groping at each other, we made our way to the living room. Stripping as we walked to the couch, she proceeded to pull me down on top of her. I felt like I was a teenager, unsure of what I was doing. She proceeded to find my now-erect penis and started to play with it as I moved on top of her. I let myself sink into the sensations, getting more excited at every caress.

A few minutes later, she looked at me and said, "We need a drink." She got up and, seeing my disappointed face, said, "I'll be right back," as she winked at me.

I laid there on my side, watching this naked, hot, sexy woman walk away. Laying on the couch, naked, I thought about what she would do to me when she came back. Then, I heard these moaning noises coming from the kitchen. I wondered what they were.

Getting up from the sofa, I walked into the kitchen. Getting closer, I could hear kissing and moaning. Now, I was thinking that maybe she was married; it had to be her husband!

Slowly, I looked around the corner. There she was, making out with a girl around my age! I quietly watched for a couple of minutes, stroking my hard cock, when she saw me and motioned for me to join them.

I was fully erect and very horny. I walked over to them, and she introduced me to her companion. "This is Misty, my stepdaughter." Misty wore an almost-sheer t-shirt that barely covered her ass. She was not wearing a bra, not that she needed one. Her nipples were dark and extremely hard. She had long, strawberry blonde hair and killer green eyes.

As I reached out to shake Misty's hand, she reached for my hard cock and gave it a squeeze. I moaned and said, "Nice to meet you." I thought I would come as she held on to me. But soon she let her hand drift down and turned her attention back to Dawn.

We stood there, in her kitchen, chatting for a bit while I tried to figure out what was happening. I cannot remember what we talked about. I was too busy convincing myself to stay cool, calm, and to just go with the flow. Oh, what a story I would have for my friends!

A short while later, Misty said that she was going to leave us so we could have our playtime and headed up to bed. We returned to the living room with our drinks in hand. I was looking forward to feeling Dawn's warm body on top of mine. I could see her wet lips waiting to receive me. Just the thought of it made my penis hard again.

"Well, guess you want to play some more, I see," she said as she grabbed my hand and led me upstairs to the master bedroom.

Entering her room, she begged me to go down on her. No argument here. I without bothering to walk to the bed, I knelt and slid down her body, stopping to suckle each one of her hard pencil nipples. They tasted sweet, like honey. Pushing her breasts together, I sucked on both her nipples at the same time, and I felt her as she squirted.

That was it for me. I wanted her sweet nectar. Sliding further down her body, I buried my face in her juicy pussy. Her clit was swollen, and she moaned as I sucked harder, sliding a finger inside her until I reached the spot where she needed me most. She soaked my face as she screamed with delight.

She commanded, "Do that again!"

I obliged, as I was brought up to respect those older than you. I continued to stimulate her clit, fingering her, and sucking on her swollen pussy lips. Again, she soaked my face with her sweet juices.

Guiding me up, she kissed me and pulled me onto the bed. I entered her, pushing as hard as she demanded. My balls slapped against her as I felt myself going deeper and deeper. We were wild animals, going like it was our last time.

She decided that she wanted to sit on my hard cock and ride it, rocking her hips back and forth. She grunted and groaned as I played with her erect nipples, pinching them until she squirted, and I came deep inside of her.

We lay there for a bit in each other's arms. I reach down to tease her clit. "*No,*" she said. "I don't have any pussy juice left in me."

"That's okay," I said. "Maybe I can help you make some more." I slid down, kissing her breast and stomach until my tongue reached her clit. Seconds later, I was rewarded with a loud scream and a blast of her come. I will never forget it.

We both jumped into the shower washed each other off. "Help me change the bedsheets," she said. Don't want to sleep on a wet bed now, do you?"

I smiled and shook my head. We crawled into bed falling, asleep in each other's arms.

I was woken by someone sucking my cock. I looked to my right and saw that Dawn was sleeping next to me. I then looked down and saw Misty going to town on my hardening cock.

Unsure of what to do, I whispered, "Your mom is right here!"

Misty just smiled, and she said, "This is what she likes me to do after she's had her fun. Just wait. She knows I am here. Don't you, Mom?"

Dawn stirred and answered, "What took you so long to start sucking that beautiful cock?" Then she got up, removed the sheet covering her, and straddled my face.

Who was I to argue two beautiful women that love each other and wanted to fuck my brains out? Misty moved up and sat on my hard cock. She rode it hard, rocking her hips back and forth so she could slide me as deeply as possible. The two beautiful women started to moan and make out as one rode my face and the other my hard cock.

At twenty years old, I was sure that I had died and gone to heaven. This went on for about ten minutes, at while point they both came.

"Hey handsome," said Dawn, "I want you to fuck my stepdaughter doggy style while she eats my pussy." Well, who am I to argue with two horny goddesses?

Dawn puffed up some pillows and arranged them at the head of the bed. Laying back, she spread her thighs nice and wide and started rubbing her clit. Misty got on all fours, with her ass held up high, and started to suck on Dawn's pussy

I got behind her and licked her for the first time, slipping a finger into her now-wet pussy. Finding her ready for me, I then slipped another finger inside of her and started stimulating her.

She pushed her ass toward my face as I continued to lick her. Unable to wait any longer, I moved up, grabbing her long hair, and slid my hard cock deep inside her. I fucked her for what seemed like a blissful eternity.

Dawn had soaked Misty's face several times as Misty continued to soak my cock and balls. Then Misty came hard, and I felt her quiver with the pleasure my hard dick brought her.

We all collapsed on the bed, as Misty found her way up to cuddle with Dawn. As these two beautiful women fell asleep, I slowly walked away. I admired their beauty as I dressed.

I could not wait to meet the boys to tell them all about my adventure.

The Swingers

He had always asked me to be more of a daredevil. His idea for a new adventure was always in the bedroom, but not ours. I often wondered what he would do if I said, "Yes." Honestly, even as I questioned his proposal, I was inwardly about it. But I never shared this appetite with him.

Sometimes, I felt that the real me was locked inside, fighting to get out. I decided that it was time for the real me to step out, to stop thinking of the "what ifs" and just explore the unknown. Plus, I was getting tired of hearing his refrain: "Classic woman, always thinking of the negative." I think this is easy for a man to say, as women can be so painfully cautious. But tonight, I was throwing caution to the wind.

I had put on my sexiest dress. It was tight and revealing. I felt like a fantasy. I made my way to our front door and nervously awaited his arrival, standing there like a wife from the 1950s with a drink in hand. He walked through the front door, and a handsome smile brightened up his face.

"Well, what a greeting! What do I owe for this?" He kissed me with a passion that went through my body, leaving a tingling sensation between my legs. I wanted him to make love to me right there, right then.

"Well, my love, this evening we are going on an adventure—a sexual one."

He looked at me with astonishment. It took him but a moment to hear and register what I had just said. "Really?"

I stared into his eyes, loosening my dress for him to see my lingerie. "Does this look like something I would wear if I weren't in a playful mood? Shower quickly. We leave after dinner."

Walking away I could feel the excitement building up in me. "But where are we going?" he asked. I was not going to let him know.

A whirling gust of warm air hit us as we walked out the front door. It carried a faint odour of the sycamore trees that lined the pathway. I stepped out toward the path, inhaling the succulent smell.

"All right, now will you tell me where we are going?" he asked with a hint of frustration in his voice.

I turned to look at him and realized that he was lost when he was not in control. "No, just get in the car," I said. Looking at me, he smiled and got into the car. I was in control, and he liked it.

Like all human activities, there are pros and cons to opening your bedroom. But a few basic principles can make any activity fun and foul free. There was one simple rule for tonight: if one goes, both go. I knew he would not decline such an offer.

We arrived at our destination after a car ride filled with questions that I refused to answer.

"Well, my love, we have arrived!" I said as we pulled up in front of the most elegant house on the street.

"Great. And where are we?" he asked.

I looked at him and said, "We have arrived as a couple and we are going home as one. Hold my hand and follow me. This is a night that you will not forget."

After having said this, he pulled me toward him told me that he loved me. I believed he now understood what awaited him behind the grand oak doors.

We arrived at the designated time. I knocked on the door with some hesitation, as I knew that in no time, my love would be walking away from me for some time.

An attractive woman opened the door. "Welcome come in. I am your hostess, Jennifer."

We entered the grand foyer to be greeted by a young strapping man offering us a beverage. We kindly accepted the beverages as Jennifer ushered us into the main room.

"So, seeing as this is your first time, let me give you a quick overview of the rules. The lifestyle of the average swinger is not a simple one. It can be complexed with some insecurities and uncertainties, especially during your first time. Be yourself and behave toward others like you want them to behave toward you. We want you to have fun and enjoy your time here, so partake in whatever makes you feel comfortable. You can say 'no'."

She then looked at my partner and ran a finger down his arm, saying, "I can help you if you are not sure what to do and not do."

As she walked away, I started to think that maybe I was wrong in bringing him here. Jennifer alarmed me, and I was beginning to despise her.

We started to walk around, mingling, meeting new and interesting people. I stopped him and asked, "Are you okay with this?"

His smile told me he was. "Are *you* okay with this?" he asked.

I knew that I was, but I had to let him know that I was bothered by our host. I needed to find the right words to tell him this without ruining his night. I knew that swinging would be invigorating, exciting, and that it would fulfil our fantasies, but I also knew that I was not comfortable with the idea that our host Jennifer may want my man for a few hours of pleasure.

"Are you confident enough that jealousy is not an issue?" I asked him with a slight concern in my voice.

"Jealous of what? When the night is over, we are going home together. What are you so worried about? I thought you were comfortable with this. You seemed so when we left the house."

I had to take a moment to think. "You know that I am not jealous, but Jennifer makes me uncomfortable about this sexual adventure we are about to take."

He looked at me and smiled. "Chin up. It is all going to be fine. This is our adventure to enjoy. And no matter what happens, you're the one I want to be with at the end of the night."

The room was immaculate, and it offered an amazing view of the city below. The walls were decorated with beautiful paintings in ornate frames, and the room was peppered with sumptuous marble statues. I noticed a sensual depiction of Aphrodite, who seemed to look at me with a playful gleam in her stone eye. *She would certainly love this gathering,* I thought.

Looking around the room, I could see so many different types of women, but Jennifer stuck out like a sore thumb. There was something about her that I did not trust—it was as if she was pretending to be someone else. Her friendly, good-natured, and radiating appearance had this relaxing effect on those around her.

As I people watched, I overheard the stories about our lovely hostess, Jennifer. "Did you know that when she chooses someone, he is hers every time?"

"Rumour has it that she has a power over men. They succumb to her every need!"

"She is a powerful bitch, and nobody defies her. Anyone who would try is a fool."

It made me wonder if I was right in thinking she is going to take my love from me. I would not allow this to happen. Although we were told to leave our inhibitions at the front door, I was still holding on to mine very tightly.

I stood by the ornate statue of Aphrodite and watched the guests mingle. Someone behind me said, "A penny for your thoughts?"

As I turned, I saw a magnificent man, a god-like creature who reminded me of Himeros, the Greek god of sexual desire.

"Just admiring the people," I said as I felt my cheeks flush.

He let out a laugh that came from deep within his chest. "I think you are looking to choose who you will have a new and different sexual experience with. Perhaps it will be that gentleman over there?" He pointed to an older, distinguished looking man who was standing next to a woman who had an air of elegance about her. "Are you willing to explore something new and fulfilling with him?" he asked as placed his hand on my shoulder. Smiling, he introduced himself. "I am Andres."

My body started to tingle with excitement—not for the distinguished-looking man, but for Andres. I turned and examined his body, taking in every inch of his frame, from his bulging biceps to his chiselled chest. "No, if given the choice, I would prefer a new and fulfilling experience with you."

He smiled at me and asked, "Where is your partner? You do know that you should be close to him while mingling with others?"

I looked across the room and saw him standing next to Jennifer and the couple she was chatting with earlier. "There he is," I said as I pointed across the room. "Next to the hostess." He looked across the room and smiled. "Well now," said Andrews with a devilish smile and a dark twinkle in his eyes. "Would you feel comfortable if they—your partner and the hostess—joined us upstairs?"

My body was aching to feel Andres hold me and ravish my body with his lips and tongue. I was feeling the wetness between my legs just thinking of what he would feel like deep inside of me. But I had to pull back, knowing that this would mean Jennifer would also have my partner. Could I let him feel her warmth, feel her lips on his, feel her tongue on his throbbing cock? Could I let myself go enough to let her have him for the night? Or was I afraid that she would take his soul forever?

Andres motioned for them to come over. I stood there numbly, wondering what I would say or do when they approached us.

"There you are," my love said as he gently kissed me and held me close to him. Jennifer looked at me with hatred in her eyes. "So, I see you have met my husband, Andres."

My heart dropped to my stomach; at the same time, my loins heated with desire at the thought that I could have the only thing she did not want me to have. Andres, Spanish for "born warrior who is manly and brave."

"Husband, you say?" I replied in an arrogant tone. "Yes, I have had the pleasure. And *he* would like the pleasure of knowing *me* more."

I could tell that she did not genuinely love this Andres. Her poised stance was cold, and when he reached for her, I could see that she was repulsed by his touch.

"So, Jennifer, why do you look so uncomfortable about this? Do you not want your husband to enjoy me—I mean us?"

Jennifer flushed at my provocation. I could see that she was too proud to back down.

"So," my love whispered in my ear. "Are we going to do this?"

Looking at Jennifer with the fury in her eyes and Andres standing next to her, I decided.

"Yes."

We would do this, knowing that not only would I have her man, but that I would also be going home with the one she really wanted.

"So," asked Andres, "How far are you both willing to go? Is kissing and oral sex approved, but no intercourse? Or are you wanting to experience it all?"

I knew from my research that this was called" soft swap," and it was a rule usually held by most first-time swingers. I did not hesitate to speak up. "My desire is to have Jennifer watch as you two beautiful men please me."

With this, I held both their hands and headed for the staircase. "Jennifer, are you not coming?" I asked with malice.

Jennifer reluctantly followed us up to the main bedroom. Once in the room, I decided that I would not be vague about my desires. After all, swinging is about exploring all your desires and wanting the people around you to help make them become real.

Adjacent to the king-size bed was an exquisite Victorian chair fit for a queen. I gestured for Jennifer to sit, as she was now the spectator in my world.

"So, tell me my dear, are you able to do this without feeling unfaithful?" Jennifer asked as she poised herself on the chair. Her long, silky legs were spread enough to allow us to see her sweet pink pussy, and her nipples teased the silk fabric of her dress as if they were playing peek-a-boo. "I ask, since some people are not able to have their cake and eat it too."

Walking over to the chair, I leaned over and whispered in her ear, "I will be savouring every moment as you watch."

I directed my attention to the two magnificent men standing at the foot of the bed, waiting for me to be their *chatelaine* for the night. I sauntered over to the bed, dropping my dress to the floor. My black, unlined bra and crotchless panties clung to my body like a second skin. Nonchalantly, I climbed onto the bed and perched myself up against the pillows, knowing that Jennifer had full view of my semi-naked body.

"Gentlemen, please undress," I commanded with a sexy infection in my voice. "Tonight, I am your mistress, and I desire to be pleased by both you, my love, and you, Andres."

Looking over at Jennifer, I saw that her position had not changed, her pink pussy was glistening, her lips were swollen with pleasure, and her nipples stood erect, waiting to be teased.

"Are you watching?" I asked.

She altered herself in the chair, as if she were suddenly restless. "Yes, I am."

It was then that I motioned for my two lovers to come closer to me. Andres slid his hand up my inner leg as my lover began to kiss me passionately. Andres's thumb brushed across the lips of my slit as my love took my erect nipple into his mouth, teasing me. I squirmed wanting my two Latin lovers to tease me more.

They were both all I could ever want and more. Two bodies ripped to perfection, with abdomens of steel and erect cocks that looked sculpted. My body desired to have them both. I grabbed their erect cocks and said, "Let me suck you both."

I raised my body up to meet their manhood. Gently, I sucked on my love's erect penis and teased it with my tongue as I squeezed Andres's cock, feeling it pulsating in my hand. I could see Jennifer watching emotionlessly. Her eyes were dark as coal, but her hands gripped the armchair as if she were holding on for life. Her displeasure excited me more because I knew that it is I who now had the power.

My love's hand reached against the back of my head as he pushed his cock deeper into my mouth. With my free hand, I grabbed his buttock, holding him close and tantalizing his anus with my index finger. He moaned in pleasure. Releasing his penis from my mouth, I start to tease his balls with my tongue.

My pleasure arousing, I released my hold of Andres and raised myself to my knees as I continued to play with my love until he came. I then shifted my attention to Andres's erect cock. I kissed the tip, then I ran my tongue along his entire shaft until I reached the tip again and guided him into my wet mouth. His body stiffened, and I pulled him closer as my mouth devoured his cock.

My love, erect once again, approached me from behind and guided himself into my wet pussy. His thrust reached my g-spot again and again until I came. Andres moaned, his cock pulsating. Before he can come, I released my mouth and pushed him onto his back. I pulled away from my lover and sat on Andres's erect cock as I guide my lover to my back door. Gently, they fucked me in rhythm, two beautiful bodies wet with sweat. I closed my eyes as my body reached levels of euphoria that I never knew. My body swayed with their every move, and every nerve in my body tingled until I screamed in ecstasy.

Jennifer remained seated, looking at us as if in a trance. I dismissed my two lovers and called her over to me. Hesitantly, she raised herself from her seat.

"Undress," I commanded. She released the straps of her gown, exposing herself to me. "Lick me," I said as I lay there with my legs apart. Without pause, she spread my legs wider and started to suck on my swollen clit her tongue. She teased my pussy, slowly licking my juices and that of my two lovers dry. She fucked my pussy with her tongue as she straddled my ass with her hands and teased it with two fingers.

Her tongue went deeper and deeper into my pussy, then out to suck my clit again as she brought her hand to tease my pussy. My body arched I yell out, "'I'm coming, I'm coming!"

She stops. I pulled her toward me, kiss her, and rolled her over. "I am the mistress here, not you."

I placed my wet pussy on hers and grab her nipples with my fingers. I grinded her until I can feel her clit pulsating next to mine, wanting to come. Almost there, I could feel myself coming, but I held on until I knew that she was close. Then, I raised myself to her awaiting mouth, wanting her to suck my pussy dry. I reached back to find her wet pussy and inserted two fingers into her until we both came. My body buckled, and I fell over beside her.

I looked over and saw my love sitting at the edge of the bed with a smile on his face. He reached out for me, and I crawled across the bed to his waiting arms.

"Here, put your dress on. Let us go home."

I turned and looked at Jennifer and Andres, two beautiful beings lost in their own world of lust.

The omecoming

He never came back. Or if he did, he never let her know. There had been no official homecoming, yet the spare key remained hidden in the rock in the garden, by the plant he gave her the summer before he left.

It had been months since they saw each other and along the way, they lost touch. He found it hard to be without her, but he thought it easier to tell her that he no longer wanted her in his life. He had the time to think it through, but she would never know that he had come to a decision. She remained in uncertainty, and the key remained where she had left it months earlier.

As she was looking at the rock, she heard a faint "hello" coming from behind her. In her heart, she had hoped it was him. Closing her eyes, she turned to see a man standing there, but he was not the one she wanted.

"Hey stranger, long time no see," she said as she approached to give him a hug. They had gone to high school together and lost contact after college. They reconnected years earlier when she saw him at the coffee shop he owned, but as life went on, they lost contact again.

"You look as beautiful as the last time I saw you," he said as he held on to the hug a little longer than she would have liked.

She invited him in for a drink, saying they should catch up on lost time. They chatted for what seem liked hours. "I guess I should get going. Don't want to wear out my welcome," he said as he stood to walk away.

Without knowing whether it was the wine or the loneliness that took over, she grabbed his arm and pulled him close to her.

He did not hesitate to return the passionate kiss she gave him. She could feel the warmth of his tongue on hers, his warm hands pulling her closer to him, and his erection rubbing against her. She let out a slight moan.

"Oh, so you like the feel of my hard cock against you? Would you rather feel it deep inside you?" he asked as he started to undress her in front of the open window.

"Humm, maybe we should close the curtains first," she said. His devilish smile told her that was not going to happen.

She caught a glimpse of herself in the window and could only think, *this is not right*. She pulled away from his arms.

"Hey, what's wrong?" he asked as he backed away from her.

"You need to leave," she said as the tears started to build in her eyes.

"No, I want to stay here. I want to feel you again," he said, reaching out to her.

"Leave, please leave." She grabbed his arm walking him to the door. "Don't come back. I cannot be with you when all you want is my body. I need someone who wants my heart."

She opened the door and watched him walk away. What had she just done?

Poring herself a glass of wine, she decided that it was time to remove the key from the rock and accept that her old love was not coming back to her. Standing in the middle of the garden with her arms open, she started to twirl around. Part of her hoped that if she twirled fast enough, she could twirl herself out of the garden and into the lush forest beyond the fence.

Falling to the ground, she looked up to see an opening in the trees and stared at the clouds as they slowly faded into each other to create a new shape of their own. She stood up and decided that it was her time to create something new for herself. She could no longer wait. She kept waiting for him to prove he still cared that he would still come home, but it had been too long. He had not given her any word of his return, so she chose to do what she needed to do. She had to become someone he knew—someone he did not know. She needed to stop playing it safe.

Grabbing the key from the rock, she took one last look at the garden they once shared. Then she started to tear it apart, uprooting the plants they had nurtured together, destroying the bench they used to sit on. Within an hour, she had torn what was once their lush hideaway garden and turned it into a pile of waste. She thought about setting it ablaze, but she decided that it would attract unwanted attention.

Walking back into the house, she took one last look at the now-ruined garden. Then she closed the door behind her.

"Guess I'll be calling a landscaper tomorrow," she said aloud as she walked to her room, glass of wine and bottle in hand.

The morning sun woke her. As she woke up, she realized that she had destroyed a piece of her past the night before. She had to face it in the daylight.

As she raised herself out of bed, the room began to spin. Getting a hold of herself, she stood up and walked down the stairs. She stopped abruptly when she saw a man standing in her ransacked garden.

Opening the patio door to see who he was, she could not help but admire his silhouette in the morning sun. He stood at least 1.9 metres tall, with shoulders as wide as her doorframe. She could see the defined muscles under his white, fitting t-shirt. His hair shined like gold in the sunlight. She could feel herself getting wet just by looking at him.

Oh, how her sexual desires were building up! She had not felt this way since her old love had left. She wanted to feel his familiar body close to hers, but he was not coming back to her. A realization she had to accept.

"Good morning," he said. "Hope you don't mind that I let myself into your garden. I tried knocking, but there was no answer."

She stood there, at a loss. "I'm sorry, but you are…?"

"Yes, I am Mario. I received your email last night about a garden in need of repair. Looking at the mess before me, I am guessing your email did not even begin to explain the help you need."

She was confused, but she politely asked, "Email? I sent you an email last night?"

"Yes, you did. Here, take a look," he said as he handed her his phone.

I must have had more to drink than I remember, she thought. She did not remember writing the email.

"Well," she said, "I guess your services are very much needed. Please feel free to walk around. I just need to freshen up. I'll come find you and let you know what I can do for you." She smiled.

"Yeah great. That will be just fine," he said. He smiled back at her as she walked to the house. Walking past the hallway mirror, she got a quick glimpse of herself. She was shocked by the woman who looked back at her. She looked like something the cat dragged in! She definitely needed to clean herself up.

She decided to use the shower in the guest room on the main floor. Turning it on, she undressed as she waited for the water to warm up. God, that landscaper was so handsome, and she was so horny. She needed to get a grip.

Walking under the stream of hot water, she grabbed hold of the shower head and sprayed her face to wake herself up. The warmth of the water running down her body, lingering on her erect nipples, aroused her even more. Cupping her breast with one hand, she lowered the shower wand between her legs. Teasing her clitoris with the warm water, she could feel her body tingling. Lowering her hand from her cupped breast, she raised her leg to rest on the shower bench and teased her vagina with her fingers.

The sensation of the warm water and her fingers was stimulating her. She could feel her heart beating faster, her blood boiling, and her pussy pulsating with every touch of her hand and the warm sensation of the water. God, she wanted *more*; she wanted to feel something more.

Mario walked by the guest bathroom. He looked into the window and, to his surprise, he could see her having her shower. He watched her body arch as she slowly teased herself with both hand and water.

He could feel his cock getting hard as he continued to watch her. Unzipping his pants, he grabbed his cock and began to stroke himself, matching her every move. God, how he wanted that woman, to feel his cock slide in and out of her as she teased herself with the water.

He walked around to the patio door and found his way to her. Stripping as he watched her, felt the overwhelming urge to feel her skin, to taste her, to be inside her. He approached the shower, and their eyes met. He saw her momentary surprise, and then he saw her eyes become inviting. He saw that she shared his hunger. As he entered the shower, he surrounded her with his body and cradled her. Sighing, she shifted her body to be as close to him as she could. Feeling his erect cock pressing against her buttocks, she turned and brushed her lips against his wet bare chest.

A dream, she thought to herself. It had been so long since felt a man so close to her. He smelled so good. He felt so warm. Everything about him overwhelmed her. If she could only feel this for a moment, she would take it.

His hands glided along her back, to her buttock, as she arched up against his wet body. Her legs parted as he lifted her up, his cock teasing her clit as he held her. She could feel him throbbing and yearned to feel him deep inside of her. Face to face, he gently kissed her as he gazed into her eyes. His warm tongue teased hers as she felt his fingers parting her lips. His firm, full cock was twitching. She groaned and rubbed up against him. He entered her with one thrust, sending shock waves through her body.

She had long been wanting to feel this sensation again. He held onto her waist, lifting her up and down, her erect nipples rubbing against his warm, wet chest. *Oh,* how she did not want this feeling to end! She could feel the blood rushing through her body with every movement he made. She had not been this close to a man in so long that she had almost forgotten that she could feel this way.

Thrusting harder and harder, she knew that she could no longer hold on. Her body released itself. She held onto him hard, her nails digging deep into his back, as she rode one orgasm after another. She could feel his body tensing up and knew that he was ready to come. Holding on to her with one hand and bracing himself on the shower wall with the other, he exploded deep inside of her. She knew that she had needed to feel a man deep inside her. She knew what it was like to need to feel like a woman, but she had never felt like *this*.

Slowly, he released his grip on her and picked up the shower wand, which was now on the floor. He slowly turned her around, so her back faced his chest, and began to tease her with the wand. Holding on to the wall in front of her, she stood on her tiptoes as he held her close with one hand and continued teasing her with the wand. The water, still warm, was brushing against her throbbing pussy. She arched her back, rubbing her wet ass against his cock. She could feel him growing.

His lips brushed against the nape of her neck as he whispered, "Let me take you from behind."

"Hmm, oh, oh," she moaned as he entered her from behind while teasing her pussy with the shower wand. Her legs were begging to give, and he could feel her stepping down from her tiptoes. Reaching ahead of her, he turned the water off. Picking her up from behind, he carried her to the bed and positioned her on her belly. He held her legs together between his and entered her again. Her body moved with hunger as she pushed herself up against him, allowing him deeper inside of her. His hands held her hips steady as she took him deeper and deeper inside of her. Together, they came in the heat of the morning.

In so many ways, this is what she needed. But at the same time, she felt that it was wrong. She felt like she had betrayed her lost love. She wanted him home, but she also needed to know that she was still a desirable woman.

Mario turned his head and pressed his lips against her cheek. "I have a quote for your garden, but I am thinking that maybe we can work it out in trade" he said as his fingertips slowly moved down her spine.

A strange moan escaped her lips as she rolled over to look at the strange man she had just had sex with. The sound of his voice sent shivers through her body. "Well then, let's start trading," she said.

The arrangement that she made with Mario was utterly unexpected, but it was the one she needed. She knew that once the garden was done, she would replace the key under its old rock, in case her love ever come home to her. Once the garden was done, she would let Mario have her for one last journey, knowing that it would be the last journey with any man other than the one whose return she hoped for.

Love

The Nomad	41
The Elevator	57
The Fool	75
The Writer	89
The Goodbye	101
The Interviews	107
The Next Chapter	111

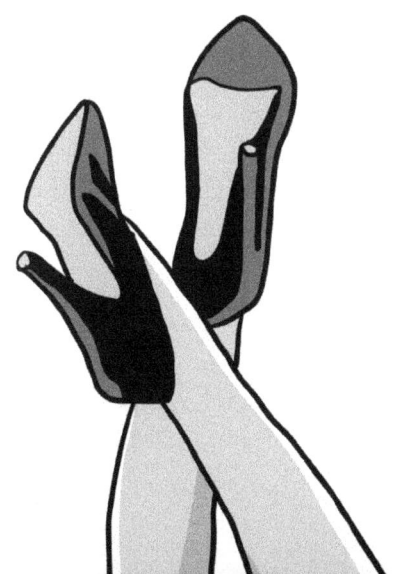

The Nomad

"Last call for flight 811, boarding at Gate 7," and the announcement rang on the airport intercom. He ran so that he would not miss his flight.

If he were lucky, this would be his last flight for work. This was a promise he had made her a few days before. "I promise that you will be with me soon. Just let me get settled and find a place for us."

Now, crossing the ramp to board the plane, he wondered if leaving her behind had been the right decision. He barely glanced back at her when she had dropped him off at the airport. It was too hard for him—he knew that if he had looked, he would have cried.

He found his seat on the plane and sat down next to a window looking out at the beautiful city he was leaving. He wondered again whether he had made the right decision.

His thoughts were disturbed by the pilot, who was announcing the take-off on the intercom. Then another voice, this one much closer, caught him off guard.

"Business or pleasure?" asked the gentleman sitting next to him.

"Business," he said.

"Me too, but I hope to find some pleasure in it," the gentleman said with a chuckle in his voice. "I'm Tony, by the way. I'm an analyst from one of the city's corporate finance institutes."

"Pleasure to meet you, Tony." He smiled, and then he turned his head back toward the window.

The plane took off. Looking out the window, he wondered which car below was hers. By now, she would be heading home, where she would be alone. He started to miss her more intensely.

"Not too bad for a sixteen-hour flight," said Tony. "Best of luck! And enjoy your time here." He smiled and walked off the plane.

Alone again, the lonely traveller started gathering his things. He walked down the slender aisle and made his way to the door.

"Sir, you forgot your laptop," said the stewardess.

Thanking her, he picked up the laptop and walked off the plane, into unknown territory. The airport was larger than he expected, and it was full of lost people running around. Finding his way outside, he took a deep breath and looked for a cab to take him to the start of his new adventure.

He had worked in many places during his twenty years as an oil-field consultant. He had worked with beautiful women, slept with beautiful women, and had known many beautiful women before. But the woman he had left behind was not just beautiful—she was lovely. At least she seemed that way to him. Her skin was a fair hue, her blue eyes sparkled like the sun on the rippling water, and her blonde locks cascaded around her shoulders… But most of all, he loved her smile. Her smile could light up a room. Although she was petite in stature, she was a strong woman.

It should have been uncomplicated to leave without worrying or missing her, but it was not. He knew that this was going to be hard and that eventually, he would have to come to terms with the knowledge that he would hurt her, even if it was only for a while. But he knew that she would still be there when he got home.

Pressure gathered in his chest as he tried to compose himself before the meeting. He had called her to tell her he arrived safely, and he could hear the sadness in her voice.

Later that night, he found that he was unable to sleep without her next to him. This did not help his composure.

As he walked into the project headquarters, he heard what seemed like the end of an argument.

"Damn it, Carlos, can you not just give me one day without shitty news?"

The man who said these words paused and turned to see the new arrival. "Oh, sorry, didn't see you there. I am Juan. Juan Garcia, CEO of Marciano Power and Energy. You the new guy who got suckered into this project?" he asked as he gave him a friendly pat on the back. "Welcome, we can use a new set of eyes and a voice of reason."

The three men sat in the stuffy boardroom for over two hours, discussing how the project could move forward with so many barriers in their way.

"The owner of the oil field is waiting to meet with us, and we need answers before we can see him. Any ideas of what bullshit we can feed him until we can find a solution for the delay?" asked Juan.

When he was met with silence, Juan decided it was now or never. He gestured for the three men to get up.

The traveller strode down the hallway with his new colleagues, knowing that he had to come up with a solution before they met with the owner. He had seen this problem before on one of his jobs in Iraq.

Iraq was where he had first met her. It had happened on the job site. He had been shocked that a woman was working in a country so dominated by men, but he saw her strength and her will to succeed, and he knew that nobody was going to mess with her. He remembered walking up to her, standing on the steps of the makeshift office, and narrowing the gap between them. He could smell the freshness of her body. It reminded him of the sweet fragrance of jasmine from the Aeranthes grandiflora orchid, which he would later learn was her favourite flower.

"Can I help you?" she had asked. For a moment, he was too mesmerized to introduce himself. He saw the devilish smile and the twinkle in her eye. He remembered scanning her body and taking in her outfit. She wore tight-fitting blue jeans and a flower shirt with rolled-up sleeves that outlined her breasts. In that moment, he had thought about how he wanted to pull her close to him and lick her breasts after making love to her. Even after all these years, his cock was getting hard just thinking about it. But he was snapped out how his reverie.

"Hey, stop daydreaming! Let us just get this over with, shall we?" said Juan as they exited the building and got into the cars that waited to take them to the owner. "We need you to do your magic," he said, as they drove away.

Sitting in the car, his mind started to wander back to Iraq. He thought of her as they drove to the nearby bar, where they had arranged to meet the owner. Jet lag had finally caught up to him so he knew it would be a good excuse to leave early. He wanted to talk to her before he slept.

The bar was a quaint place with a country feel. There were round wooden tables with less-than comfortable chairs. The bar ran along the four walls of the room. The place was filled with people of all age groups.

In the corner, he saw a man dressed like a pimp—he wore a red velvet suit with a leopard collar and a homburg hat. To his right, there was a woman in a skimpy shiny purple dress that barely left anything to the imagination. She had an exhausted appearance, as if she had been suffering for a long time. Her body sat in a graceless manner, as if she were unable to move unless she was pushed.

"Hey, if you're looking for a night of fun, she may be the one," said Juan.

Smiling, he thanked him for the offer but declined it. "You never been with a prostitute before, my friend?" Juan asked in a jovial voice. "Remember that a prostitute is like a fantasy. She will do whatever you want. Things that your wife or girlfriend would say no to. She must do what you ask. She has no choice. Am I right Carlos?"

"Yes, sir, you are," said Carlos, laughing. "Now, let's get some liquor into us before the owner arrives."

The traveller laughed inwardly. Little did his companions know that the beautiful woman waiting for him at home was adventurous. She was his fantasy come true. He did not need a prostitute or any other woman so long as he had her, but he did not share this with them.

They did not know or need to know, but he *had* had sex with a prostitute when he was in his twenties. He had been working in the desert for longer than he could remember. It had been months since he had had sex, and his co-workers told him of a brothel that had all the elegant whores in the region.

During his first visit, he met a tall woman with an olive complexion and emerald-green eyes. She was not what you would call attractive, but she had an elegance about her. Every time he had time off, he would arrange to spend a night with her. After sex, she would lay there next to him and listen to his secrets. He was enthralled by her attentiveness. Being so young, he believed that he was in love with her. Then, one day, she told him that she could no longer spend time with him. She said that she did not want to be attached to anyone, that her job was her life, and that she enjoyed it. He was hurt by her words and never returned to the brothel.

"Daydreaming again?" asked Carlos. "FYI, the owner had called to say he can't make it. We must reschedule for tomorrow. Meet us at the construction site first thing in the morning, say 9:00 a.m."

Tired after his first day in a new town, he was glad to hear this, as he wanted to leave so he could call her.

"So, my friend, are you sure you don't want a companion for the night?" asked Carlos.

"No, I am good. I must leave before I fall asleep here on this table."

He said his goodnights and left. Arriving at his hotel, he checked the time to see if she would be back from work. He decided to shower before he called her.

She had been working for the family business since college. It was a world-renowned company that had been started by her grandfather. Even so, she had never had the luxury of being given a job—she had to apply, just like everyone else. Her grandfather never believed in family favours—he believed in hard work. Hard work is how she showed her grandfather that she could do as much work as her father and brother.

During her college days, she had vowed that she would never work for the family. All that changed when her college friend, Stephan, derived a plan that would change the way her family ran their business, with all their hidden secrets. Together, she and Stephan worked on projects that would take them to places that were not welcoming to women or gay men. This was an eye-opener for the family, who knew the dangers they could face but understood their reasoning. Most of all, they hoped that the family secrets would not be revealed.

It was on one of these contracts that she met him. She still remembered the way he looked at her on the steps. Right away, she had known that he was attracted to her.

It was his first day on the project, and she was happy to see a new face—especially one as handsome as his. They went about the day, and she introduced him to the project. By evening, it was clear that he needed a rest.

"Want a cold drink?" she asked.

He smiled, saying, "Sure."

She brought him back to the office, where she pulled out a bottle of Arak. Pulling two glasses from her drawer, she proceeded to pour them each a glass. "I thought you said a cold drink," he said.

"Oh yeah, you're right." She walked over to the mini fridge and grabbed some ice. Dropping the cubes into their glasses, she said, "There you go, a cold drink."

"You know liquor is against the law in this country?" he said.

"Yes, it is but so is premarital sex, and look," she said as she pointed to the young men waiting for the bus ride to the camp. "Do they look sexually deprived to you? Well, they are, but they are off to a secret brothel. Getting laid once a month makes them more productive," she said with a smile on her face.

Laughing, he thought to himself, *She is one tough bitch.*

They sat drinking for a bit, and then she asked him, "Are *you* sexually deprived? Because if you are, the bus to the brothel will be leaving in less than 10 minutes."

She had caught him off guard. He did not know what to say when she stood up, approached him, kissed his cheek, and then took a step back to admire him. "It's no problem if you are sexually deprived, because I am, and there hasn't been a good-looking man around here until today."

With these words, he grabbed her arm, pulling her toward him, and kissed her. She responded to his kiss without hesitation. "Come with me," she said as she led him to the roof of the office.

The sky was littered with stars, and you could hear the silence. She proceeded to unbutton his shirt exposing his muscular chest. Slowly, she kissed his chest, working her way to the waistband of his jeans. Unfastening the buckle of his belt, he stopped her. "What if we get caught? We will be executed!"

"Well, at least you would die with a smile on your face," she said.

In that moment, he knew that he would spend the rest of his life with her.

The phone rang numerous times before she answered.

"Hey, how are you?" he asked.

"I am good. I miss you," she said as she sat down on the bed.

"What took you so long to answer the phone?" he asked.

She sighed and shifted her position on the bed. "I was getting a glass of wine. Can't sleep without you here."

His heart felt a twinge of pain knowing how lonely she was without him. "I will see you soon. Twelve weeks is not that long." But he knew twelve weeks was too long.

"When you come home to me, I am taking you away. Kidnapping you so that you're mine and only mine forever. I'm going to take you to the cabin and seduce you."

He smiled listening to her words and asked, "What are you going to do to me?"

She started to tell him. "I am going to kiss you. Holding your face in my hands, I will kiss you deeply and passionately. I will unbutton your shirt and feel the warmth of your chest under my hands. I will kiss your chest till I reach your jeans, and I will unzip them till I find your hard cock. Slowly, I will kiss your cock from the tip to the base. My mouth will open wide to take you in slowly. My warm mouth will be filled with red wine. I will savour you and the wine together.

"I will stroke you with my hand as my tongue slowly teases the tip of your penis. I will not stop until I feel you wanting to release in my mouth. Cupping your balls, I will move my lips up and down your shaft until you explode in my mouth. Raising myself, will I kiss my way back up to your mouth and let you taste your sweetness and the wine on my lips. I will tell you that I want to feel you, to engulf you, to be one with you, and I will remove my clothes.

"Standing naked in front of you, I'll anxiously wait for you to bury your face between my legs. Your warm tongue will tease my clit with enthusiasm, and your fingers will slide in and out of me with a steady rhythm. I will cry out in pleasure, and my back will arch as I reach my first orgasm, holding your head close between my legs so you can feel my juices run down your mouth. Slowly, I will guide you back up to me and remove the rest of your clothing to feel your naked body close to mine.

"Your cock will be hard again, waiting to enter me. I will push you on the bed and I lower myself onto you, feeling the sensation of your hard cock filling me. My body will tremble, but I will not want to come yet. I will hold on to your shoulders as I fuck you slowly, feeling your hard cock deep inside of me. You will pull my face to yours and kiss me while I ride you harder. Our bodies will move together in rhythm, like a dance, as another wave of orgasmic pleasure will hit me. You will grab my arms and hold them behind my back, firmly arousing me even more. Then you will thrust deeper and deeper inside me, rapidly causing my breast to bobble up and down as my pussy throbs for more. I will throw my head back as I continue riding you, adding a layer of euphoria to my already heated body. I will scream as my body releases one more orgasm for my love.

"You'll flip me over on my back, your eyes wide open, your face glistening with beads of sweat like a wolf coaching his prey. I will moan with excitement as I anticipate my next orgasm. You will enter me slowly, parting my flesh with your warm, hard cock. I will raise my legs over your shoulders so I can feel you deeper inside of me. You will kiss me as you thrust deeper and harder. As my arms hold on to you, I will moan with pleasure into your mouth. Each stroke will be more intense. You will grab my arms and hold them over my head as you fuck me harder and deeper. I will have an orgasm after another until together, we will come.

"You'll hold me tight for a few minutes, and I'll lay my head on your chest and listen to the beat of your heart. Then you will roll over onto your back, your eyes closed and a smile on your face."

After she finished, we were silent for a moment.

"Sweetheart are you still there?" she asked.

"Yes, I am here."

"Good," she said, "Thought I scared you away."

"No. If anything, you gave me a reason to come home sooner."

Tantalizing Desires

He slept well that night, dreaming of their conversation, knowing that he had a good reason to go home. She was that reason. Every little thing about her made him want her more. Her curly, blonde, unkempt hair, her smile (which makes everyone smile), her precious blue eyes, and her frankness, which sometimes got her in trouble. She was his dream come true. She was someone who loved him and never doubted him. God, how he wanted to be there with her. He was tempted to call in sick, but he knew that he needed to worry about the job. And he knew that he had to meet the owner at 9:00 a.m. He sighed and got ready for the day ahead.

When he got to the job site, he was still frustrated. It looked like every other job site he had worked on. He did not understand why they needed him here.

"So, what do you think?" asked Carlos as he approached him. "Damn nice piece of land, isn't it?"

He looked around to see that the land stretched out for miles. A tree-scattered background went on for miles. As he continued to look at the landscape, he noticed a man looking out of place, standing in the middle of the field. There was nothing in front of him, but he almost looked like he was staring at a stranger.

"Who the fuck is that?" he asked with an air of concern.

Carlos answered, "He is the problem that you need to fix. Remember, before the meeting, I asked what bullshit we could feed the owners? Well, we need to find that bullshit."

"Well, come on, now. Come hear his story and see what you can do."

Together, they walked to middle of the field. As they approached, they saw that the elderly man had a basket at his feet. Carlos motioned for him to start talking and took a step back to listen.

The elderly man's face was familiar, but he could not place where he had seen this face before.

"Sir, may I help you?" he asked.

The elderly man tuned to look at him and, with a stern tone, he asked, "Please, sir, get off my land and bring back my flower."

It was then that he realized that there would be trouble. He looked at Carlos and asked, "His flower? And is this his land?"

Carlos shrugged his shoulder, replying, "Flower is his daughter. And as for the land, yes and no. He did own the land, but he lost it in a bet. The winner of the bet then sold the land to us, on the condition that a percentage of the profits would go to his only daughter, Flower. The problem is that we cannot bring Flower to him, so until then, our hands are tied. That is, unless you can do your job and convince him to let us start digging. He knows that there are millions of dollars headed her way, but he won't budge."

This job was proving to be anything but simple. Leaving the old man behind, they headed back to the makeshift office to meet with the owner. He still could not shake the feeling that he somehow knew this man.

"Good morning, gentlemen, I bring fresh coffee and sweetbread!"

Recognizing the voice, he turned around. It was Tony, the gentleman he sat next to on the plane.

"Well, we meet again! I am gathering that you are our troubleshooter," said Tony as he extended his hand. "I also gather that you have met our problem," he said as he pointed to the elderly man on the field.

"Yes, I have, and it will be a simple solution if we can just find his daughter."

Tony and Carlos looked at each other before turning their attention back to him. "Well," said Carlos, "We know where his daughter is, who she is, and what she is. Do you remember the woman sitting in the corner with the pimp at the bar last night? Well, she is the old man's daughter and the pimp's companion."

"Ah shit!" he said, wondering out loud. "We need to figure out how to get her away from him."

"The only solution is to buy her for the night, but no man is willing to pay for her," said Tony.

"And no man is willing to sleep with her either," said Carlos.

He knew there was more to this story than what they were telling him, but he did not care. He just wanted to find a solution so he could go home.

They were back at the bar that night, and he saw her sitting there. She was in the same spot and she wore the same dress. He could see the desolation in her eyes, but at the same time, he saw a cry for someone to look close enough and save her. She had a story. But he had a job and no time for her story.

What the fuck can I do? he asked himself.

Her story was simply that of a young girl falling in love with an older man. She believed that he loved her as much as she loved him.

From a young age, she had a gift that many people thought to be evil and others, a gift of prosperity. She had the mind of a psychic, which gave her the ability to predict tomorrow and all the tomorrows after that. Her father always saw it as a gift to make them rich and comfortable; to her lover, it was an asset one could use to gain control.

Flower was born into a poor family during the festival of spring. Her gifts started to shine as she became a young girl. Her family treasured her gift, and they gained much wealth from them over the years, but these gifts stopped the day she met Tamas. Tamas was a traveller whom she met at the local market. Their eyes met, and she knew that she wanted to be his forever.

She found a way to introduce herself to him, and they spent every hour together after that. One star-filled night, he kissed her. This was her first kiss. She wanted more kisses so she could feel more, but her gift seemed to be lost when she was with him. Tamas pretended to love her and married her to gain possession of her gift. He used her gift to manipulate everyone around him. Even as he stole from them, he promised to make them rich. Flower knew that he did not love her like she loved him, but she could see all her tomorrows and knew it would be safer for her to remain with him. Her gift was now a curse for her. With this knowledge, she withdrew into herself.

"Carlos, Tony, watch my back," he said as he walked over to Flower.

"Excuse me miss, may I have a word with you?" he asked.

Tamas stood up and asked who he was.

"I am just one of the people working on her father's old land, and I need to speak with her about some family business."

She looked at him, and he could see some life coming back into her eyes. He knew that she missed her father.

"Any of her business comes through me," said Tamas.

"Fine. It's quite simple. I need her to visit her father so that we can move along with our project.".

Tamas's dark eyes stared at her. He asked, "Is this your tomorrow?"

She said, "No, but he knows who my tomorrow is." Tamas walked away as if he had lost a battle.

"I will meet with my father," said Flower as she lifted herself off the bar stool. "Thank you for brining me my tomorrow," she said as she walked in the direction of Carlos and Tony.

He did not understand what she was saying, but he didn't care—now, he could move along with the project and get home to the woman he genuinely loved and missed.

Leaving the bar, he went back to his hotel room. "I am coming home soon," he said on the phone. "Will you still be there for me?" he asked.

She could barely contain her tears when she heard his voice telling her he was coming home. He was finally coming home. "Yes, I am here for you," she said as the tears ran down her cheeks. "Where else would I be?"

Flower knew that what happened at the bar the night before must have been a dream, but when she woke, Tony was still laying there next to her. She could feel the warmth of his body, and she could smell his scent.

When she reached out to touch him, he awoke and smiled at her. His hand gently touched her back, the tips of his fingers outlining her scars. As he continued to touch her body, she shifted closer to him. She parted her legs as he positioned his body over her. His throbbing cock wanted to get deep inside of her and feel her moistness.

She grabbed his cock and guided him to her wet pussy. He moaned with pleasure as he slid deep inside of her. She pulled him closer to her. Reaching to find her clit, he teased her and whispered in her ear, "We will be together forever."

She moved her body in time with his, hungry for his throbbing cock. "Deeper, deeper," she moaned, and he obliged.

A strange moan escaped her lips as he pinched her clit. With every thrust, her body was aching for more. Her nipples grew sensitive to the air around them.

"Harder, harder!" she screamed as they came together.

If, in his life, there was a night that he wished he could live again, it would have been the first night he had with her. He looked at her across the living room. She was no longer that graceless looking woman sitting in a corner. She was his.

"Tony are you ready?" asked Flower. "We need to go."

Tony got up, walked over to her, and kissed her passionately. He said, "We always have tomorrow."

The levator

As soon as he heard the job offer, he knew that could not decline it. Even though he promised his wife that she could go with him this time, he knew that it would not be possible. This job, like many others, would take him away for months.

Despite his travelling, he still taught himself to keep in shape. His morning routine never changed: wake up, brush teeth, wash face, put on the shorts and t-shirt she had given him years ago, and put on his favourite runners.

Every morning, he would get on the elevator at the same time, and there she was, as if she were waiting for him.

"Good morning," she said with a smile. She was a slender woman with long black hair and big brown eyes. He guessed that she was in her mid- to late-thirties. She was always dressed in a pencil skirt, a peekaboo blouse, and black heels. Her breasts would peek out over her white lace bra.

"Good morning," he said as he adjusted himself in the hopes that she would not see his cock getting hard. He stood next to her, close enough to smell her sweet perfume.

He remembered what his wife had said to him when he left home. "The realm of a fantasy can spread wide, and you will find the freedom to meet many new people. You have your weekly meeting away from the work site, in a completely different town, many miles away. There will be empty hotel rooms in which you will feel so lost, wishing I was there to share your free time with you. But in reality, you will be alone. You'll want to cheat because you'll know that you can."

Back in the elevator, followed her out of the opening doors, watching her hips move side to side in a rhythm of their own. She glanced over her shoulder with a smoldering smiling that set his loins aflame.

"Have a good day," she said as she left the building. Smiling back at her, he wondered what she felt like, what she tasted like. Gathering his thoughts, he left the building to run off his sexual frustration.

After weeks of admiring her in the elevator, he decided to throw caution to the wind and ask her out for a drink. What harm could a drink do when he knew that the woman who genuinely loved him was waiting for him at home? She would understand that it was just a drink. Even if she had warned him, before his departure, that he would feel tempted to cheat during his trip...

His thought was interrupted with an incoming call. He looked at his phone to see that it was her calling.

"Hello, how are you?" he asked.

"Horny as hell. Let us play," she said.

He laughed, saying, "Yes, let's play. Let me go to the bedroom first." As he walked to the bedroom, he could hear her faint moans on the phone. "I hear that you have started without me," he said.

"What do you want to do to me?" she asked.

He went to the bed, unzipping his jeans, and reached into his pants. His cock was semi erect, but he knew that just hearing her voice, her moans, and her seductive tone would make him hard.

"Are you naked?" he asked.

"Yes," she said with a slight moan in her voice.

"I want you to get your favourite toy and rub it along the outside of your pussy while you tease your clit." He could hear her moaning and softly calling his name. "Your dildo is my hard cock teasing your pussy then your ass. Do you like that?"

She could not speak, and he could tell that she was lost in his words. He knew that her fingers rubbed her clit as her dildo played between her wet pussy and her ass. His cock was hard, and he wanted to come, but he would wait for her.

"That's it. Now, guide my hard cock into your wet pussy."

He could hear her arch her back as the pulsating dildo reaching her G-spot.

"Oh, babe you feel so good," she said as she continued to push the dildo deeper inside of her.

"Don't come, babe, I want you to take me in your ass."

He knew that she would guide the dildo into her ass and insert two fingers into her dripping pussy.

"Ah yes, baby, it feels so good. Don't stop! Harder, baby, harder."

His cock was throbbing he was about to come, but he waited to do it with her.

"Yes, baby, yes!" Together, they came as one.

"I miss you" she said as she caught her breath.

"I miss feeling this with you here."

"I know," he said, "I will be home soon."

He could hear her sadness on the other end of the phone. He started to wonder if being away from her was even worth it.

He woke to the sun shining through the bedroom window. Walking to the bathroom, he was thinking about last night's call. He missed his wife more than he thought he would. Looking at himself in the mirror, he fiddled with the necklace he always wore. She had given it to him so many years ago. He never took it off. It was a way to have her with him, no matter how many miles kept them apart. With that thought, he was surprised by how erect he was, and he was delighted at the time they had shared the night before, even if it was just over the phone.

He quickly dressed for his morning run. Waiting for the elevator, he realized that he may see the black-haired woman again. He wondered what she would be wearing today.

As the elevator doors opened, there she stood in a stunning contour dress that outlined her hourglass figure.

"Good morning," she said.

He smiled and walked into the elevator.

"Nice morning for a run, but it may be a little difficult with that erection," she said. He glanced down and realized that he was fully erect. and He to hide it the best he could.

"Here," she said as she walked over to him. "Let me help you with that." The elevator doors were barely closed when she proceeded to kiss him and grabbed his cock.

"I will take care of this for you," she said as she got on her knees before him. She slipped his pants down and opened her mouth wide to take him slowly. He drew back up against the elevator wall, holding onto the rail for balance. He knew that this was wrong and wanted to push her away, but her warm tongue started to lick him up and down, and he was suddenly lost in her warmth.

The elevator lights began to flicker, and the elevator fan began to whine. Then, they were suddenly in darkness. Tension coiled deep inside of him, and he pushed her away.

"What's wrong?" she asked. "Are you not enjoying this?"

He fumbled until he was able to pull up his shorts. Finding his way to the panel board, he pushed the emergency button in the hopes that someone would start the elevator again and he could escape.

"Slow down," she said, "You can't get out, so let us just have some fun until we get moving again."

The emergency light turned on, and he could see her plump lips and what was left of her red lipstick. He wanted to take her and push her up against the wall, with her bottom against his groin. He approached her, forcing her face toward his and rubbing his thumb against her lush lips. She raised her hand to his chest, pulling him closer to her. Suddenly, the lights flicked back on.

"Powers back," she said as he backed away toward the door. As soon as the door opened, he raced out, not taking the chance to look back at her.

He arrived at work, anticipating that the day would be busy so that he could forget the incident in the elevator.

"Good morning," said Lynette. "Are you okay?" she asked with an air of concern in her voice.

"Yes, I am fine," he said as he rushed to his office.

Entering his office, he was greeted by Antonio, one of the investors for the project that he was working on. *Great, an interruption to my thoughts.*

"Hey, how are you?" Fernando looked up and smiled when he saw his face.

"Well, I am better than you. Why the look of guilt on your face, my friend?" he asked.

"What are you talking about? I have nothing to be guilty about."

Antonio looked at him and laughed. "Yeah, that's what they all say. Well, I do hope she was worth it."

"*No*, no it's not like that! I can explain," he said.

Antonio sat back, laughing even harder, "Fine, I am all ears. Talk away. Tell me all about it."

He began to tell his story.

Entering his apartment building, he saw her standing in the lobby waiting for the elevator. God, how he wanted to run in and push her up against the wall! He knew that she would get off on the force of his movements.

"What the fuck are you thinking?" he asked himself aloud before turning and walking away from the building. He must have been walking for a good hour before he realized that he had found himself in a part of town he did not recognize. Looking around, he found a bar nestled between a lingerie shop and a barber. Walking in, he felt like he had traveled back to 1980. The men were dressed like the backstreet boys and the women all looked like Madonna, but these people were old enough to be their parents. He took a seat at the bar and ordered a beer. Looking around, he wondered where the hell he was.

"Where are you from?" asked the man sitting two stools over. "Never seen you here before."

He initially assumed that this man was a local, but as they kept chatting, he found out that he was in fact was a foreigner, like himself.

Before he could answer, he was interrupted by a familiar voice. "So, I see you have found the only spot in this country that serves cold beer and warm imported whiskey," said Antonio. "May I join you?"

They had a few more beers and whiskey shots before he resolved to head back to the apartment and prepare for tomorrow's meeting.

"Antonio, my friend, I need to get out of here." He left before Antonio could say anything.

As he entered the apartment, the telephone rang. His screen displayed his wife's name, who was using a video chat app to call him. The tension coiled deep inside of him, as he knew that once she saw his face, she would know. She could always tell how he felt just by looking at him.

She had been that way since the first day they met thirty years ago. He remembered the first time he saw her walk into the university cafeteria, where he sat playing scopa with his friends. She was wearing an authentic seventies-inspired hippie blouse and faded blue jeans with brown leather sandals. Her curly blonde hair flowed freely around her shoulders, outlining her deep blue eyes. Her smile captured everyone who was looking at her.

He still remembered the sweet smell of her perfume as she walked by his table. As he watched her walk by, his friends said he had a look on his face that they had never seen before.

"Oh my god! He has a crush on her!" said his friend Emile. The others joined in and laughed.

"I am going to spend the rest of my life with her," he said. "That's right." he said out loud as he threw his cards onto the table.

He was jerked back to the present by the sound of the phone. As he answered her videocall, he could see that she was as beautiful today as she was the first day when he met her. He did not want to lose her.

"Hi," he said.

"Hey sweetheart. I was beginning to think you forgot about our phone date tonight."

He looked at her and wished he could reach through the screen and pull her to him. How he missed the feel of her body next to his, the sweet kisses that were always followed by a smile, the way she looked at him when he spoke…

"What happened to your necklace?" she asked. He raised his hand to his neck and realized that it was missing.

"I don't know," he said. "Maybe I dropped it in the shower this morning." But he did remember having it on when he entered the elevator that morning. "I don't know. I will have to look around for it," he said, hoping that she would accept his answer as he bit down on his lower lip and downward.

She knew him too well. Before they started dating thirty years ago, she always remembered him sitting playing scopa in the cafeteria. She would always wonder, *Does he ever go to class?*

Walking into trigonometry class, she saw him sitting in the back row so as not to be noticed. One day after class, he stopped her in the cafeteria as she walked by the table where he sat playing scopa with his friend.

"Hey," he said, "would you happen to have notes for today's lecture?"

She always remembered his brown eyes and his childlike grin. "Yes, I do," she said.

"May I have a look at them?" he asked.

She bent forward to get closer to him. She knew that he would be able to smell her sweet perfume, and she could tell that she had whisked him away. Then she spoke. "Sure, for a price," she said.

She could see the surprise in his face. "How much?" he asked.

She looked at him smiled and gave him a peck on his cheek. "I will let you know when I see you in physics class. Don't show up, and you get nothing," she said as she walked away, chuckling with her friends in tow. From the look on his face, she knew that he was hers for life.

"What happened?" she asked.

He raised his head and looked at her, saying, "I'm sorry."

They were words that she never wanted to hear, for she knew what they truly meant. Her heart fell to her stomach and she asked, "Was she worth it?" before tears started to weld up in her eyes.

Seeing her tears running down her soft cheeks broke his heart. "I never slept with her. It was just a blowjob," he said with pain in his voice. But he knew that he had hurt her.

"I have to go," she said before she disconnected the call.

He sat back looking at the blank screen asking himself, "What the fuck did I do?"

She sat there for a moment longer, looking at the blank screen, recalling the look of hurt in his eyes when he told her what he had done. She knew that he loved her, but even so, she did not know if she could forgive him. How dare he just throw that out there? Why had he not prepared her for it?

She stood up; she knew what she had to do. She headed to their room and took out her suitcase. She had no concept of what she was going to pack or why she was packing, for that matter. Sitting at the edge of the bed, she collected her thoughts.

"Where the hell am, I am going?" she asked out loud. She then fell back on the bed and cried herself to sleep.

The cool night breeze woke her. Looking around, she realized that she fallen asleep for some time. She got up and reached for the light beside the bed. As the room lit up, she saw the picture of her man. It had been taken on the night that she had given him the necklace for his birthday.

Many would think it is just a necklace, but for her it had meaning. Tears started to weld up in her eyes, but before she could wipe them away, the phone rang. She ran her hand over the phone before picking it up. She knew that it was him. Raising the phone to her ear, she composed herself, not wanting to let him know the real hurt she was feeling.

"Hello," she said in a soft voice.

" Are you okay?" he asked. When she did not respond, he just shrugged. "I understand if you don't want to talk to me. I can't change what happened, but I know that everything can go back to the way it was as soon as I get home."

His words tightened like a tourniquet around her throat. She found it hard to breathe. The tension coiled up inside of her before she found the strength respond. *It cannot be the same again,* she thought to herself. She knew how much she loved him, and she did not want to lose him. But he had crossed a line, and he could not take it back.

He cried as he continued to tell her how much he loved her. She now needed to decide if his love was enough to fix this.

He decided not to go for a run that morning, seeing as he did not sleep the night before and he had to get to the office early for a meeting. He figured he would not see the woman in the elevator this early. Yet, as the doors opened there, she stood.

"Good morning. I have been waiting for you," she said. "I have something that I think you will want."

As he started to walk away, she pulled him back into the elevator, letting the doors close behind him. As the elevator started to move, she pressed the "stop" button. She held up his necklace, asking him, "Have you been looking for this?"

He reached for it, but she pulled her hand back. "If you want it, you need to come and get it," she said as she placed it under her skirt.

He stood there, looking at her and her bewitching smile as she leaned against the elevator wall, legs spread apart. Slowly, she raised her skirt until he got a glimpse of her pink pussy.

"Come closer and get your necklace," she said. As he stepped closer, he realized that this was a mistake, but he knew that he had to get the necklace back.

"Just give it to me," he said.

She reached out to him and said, "Here." She grabbed it and placed it on her pussy. "You can use your fingers to get it out, but I would prefer you used your tongue," she said as she bit her bottom lip.

Under the flickering light, he bent down to find himself within an inch of her wet pussy. He could see her swollen clit and the chain from his necklace hanging out of her pussy. Gently, he tugged at the chain and she moaned, saying, "Lick me!"

He hesitated, then finished pulling his necklace out of her dripping pussy. Moving away from her, he said, "I can't." Then he pushed the elevator button to open the door and left.

He stood looking out the window of his office, thinking that it was all a dream—a bad dream that he wished he could wake up from. His thoughts were interrupted by a knock at the door. His office door was usually always opened; the very fact that it was closed told him that he needed to leave.

"Come in," he said.

As the door opened, he saw his wife standing there. She entered his office with her head held high. He could not believe that she was there in front of him. As he walked to her, her gaze drifted over his body. She reached out and welcomed him into her arms.

He looked at her, asking "Why did you come? I though after last night you were leaving me. I was convinced that I would never see you again. I just wanted to leave this place and get to you!" he said as he kissed her passionately.

"I see you found the necklace. Where was it?" she asked as she traced the outline of its shape against his chest.

"Doesn't matter where I found it. All that matters is that you are here."

She felt the restlessness in his touch and knew that something was bothering him. She stepped away, unsure what she should do next. Turning away from him, she could feel the tears building up in her eyes. Her heart felt like it was breaking as she stood there, knowing that something was missing between them.

"What's wrong?" he asked as he approached her from behind reaching out to take her in his arms. She wanted to tell him that she knew, but what did she really know? Was it the other woman? Was he falling for her?

Turning looking at him she said, "I can't make you stay in love with me if you don't want to, but you should at least be honest with me."

He was unable to answer her. His silence said it all, and she left him standing speechless and alone in the middle of his office. He chased her to the door.

"Stop! Please let us go to the hotel and talk."

Nodding in agreement, she followed him.

They reached the hotel after walking in silence for what seemed like a lifetime. He opened the door. Pushing him aside, she walked in and threw her luggage on the bed.

Turning around to look at him standing by the closed door, she asked, "Does she live in this building too? Will I bump into her one morning on my way out?"

"I don't know, I have only seen her a few times in the elevator and lobby."

She looked at him and laughed. "Really? you don't know?" she asked.

"I don't know. Honestly, I do not. Maybe she was visiting someone. I honestly do not know."

He heard the words coming out of his mouth and fought to find more to say, but he couldn't think of anything. He looked at her as she walked into the bathroom and closed the door. Again, she left him alone in the middle of a room, speechless.

They slept separately that night—something they had never done in all the years together. She tossed and turned trying to get the image of the other woman out of her head. Was this woman tall, short, sexy, thin? She wanted to know, for maybe knowing would tell her *why*.

She finally cried herself too asleep. She woke to find him asleep on the sofa. She wanted to cuddle up close to him and feel his warm body next to hers. She wanted to smell his scent and feel his breath on her neck. She just wanted him to love her the way he always had. Her emotions were in turmoil. She was hurt, but she needed him.

She decided that the only way to clear her mind was with a nice run. The fresh air would do her good. Looking at him lying there, she bent over, picked up the blanket, and gently placed it on him. Walking to the bathroom, she felt a tear run down her cheek.

She quietly closed the door behind her, so as not to wake him. Standing at the elevator, she started stretching and waiting. Her thoughts started to stray, and she wondered if she would ever meet this other woman. And if she did, what would she say?

As the elevator door opened, she saw a stunning woman standing inside. She was slender, with long black hair and big brown eyes. She guessed that the woman was in her mid- to late- thirties.

"Good morning," she said. Smiling and wondering if *this* was the other woman, she walked into the elevator and said "good morning" back. The elevator was old and dilapidated, and she wondered if it would make it down the six flights.

"Are you alright?" asked the woman.

"I am not sure," she said with a slight unease in her voice.

"Will this make it to the ground floor without falling?" she asked with a nervous laugh.

"Oh, it may stop along the way, as it does on occasion, but that just makes the ride more fun."

The elevator started to descend when suddenly it stopped. The emergency lights switched on, and all she could think of was the physics of how an elevator worked. *N = mg if the elevator is at rest or moving at constant velocity; N = mg + ma if the elevator has an upward acceleration; N = mg - ma if the elevator has a downward acceleration... Oh, my goodness,* she thought. *I am such a nerd.*

"Are you talking to me?" the woman asked.

She had not realized that she spoke out loud. "Sorry, no, I was just talking to myself."

"Ah, and who thinks you are a nerd?" she asked as she walked closer. "I think nerds are sexy creatures. So, I guess that makes you a sexy creature. Am I right?"

She felt her cheeks flush "Well, I will not argue with logic," she said to ease the tension when the elevator went dark.

He woke to a silent hotel room. Getting up, he looked around the room to see that she had left, but her luggage remained. This, he thought, was a good sign. Still, she was also in a strange town. He hoped that she would be careful.

He sat down on the bed, thinking of what had been said last night. He accept the fact that he needed a better perception of what had happened. He questioned himself as to whether he still loved her or wanted the freedom to have any woman.

"I need to talk to her," he said out loud as he dressed and ran out the door to look for her. He knew that he was still in love with her, and she needed to know. Approaching the elevator, he pushed the button.

"Damn, why won't this elevator start?" she asked, pushing all the buttons in the hope that they would soon be moving again only to cut her finger.

"*Stop!*" the woman said as "Look, you have hurt yourself!" she said as she grabbed her hand. "Hitting all the buttons will not make this contraption work. it will start in its own due time as it always does."

She did not let go of her hand; instead, she raised it to her mouth. "You're bleeding. Let me take care of that for you," she said as she placed her bleeding finger into her mouth.

The woman's lips were moist and warm, and her tongue was soft. She could smell the woman's sweet scent. Closing her eyes, she inhaled her smell and felt a tingling sensation between her legs.

"Are you alright?" asked the stranger in a soft voice.

The woman moved closer to kiss her. Her lips were soft, and she could taste her own blood on her tongue. She felt possessed by this woman. Slowly, the woman's hands moved up to her breasts, and she could feel her fondling her now-erect nipples as she continued to kiss her.

"May I see them?" she asked as she started to raise her top.

Without saying a word, she let the woman lift her shirt. Gently, she sucked on her nipples with little arousing bites. They kissed some more, and the woman pushed her tightly against the wall. The woman's hands found the bottom of her shorts. She reached under the fabric to grab her ass, and she fondled her butt cheeks before reaching lower to touch her throbbing, wet pussy.

The woman inserted her long finger into her with a force that made her come. Holding onto the railing, she raised herself so that she could feel the woman's finger even deeper inside of her.

"You like that?" the woman asked. "What if I stop?"

"No, please don't stop!" she said between moans of pleasure.

But the woman did stop. "Elevator's working now," she said as she arranged her clothing and picked up her handbag and briefcase.

Standing there waiting, he realized that the elevator was most likely stuck again. He took the stairs, running in the hope that he would find her quickly. As he reached the lobby, he could hear the elevator starting and decided to wait to see if she was on it.

As the doors opened, his jaw dropped. There they both stood.

"I have been looking for you," he said with a look of shock on his face. He deeply hoped that his wife did not know that the woman standing next to her was *the* other woman.

She walked out of the elevator and momentarily looked back at the creature who had just brought her to an amazing orgasm.

"Let's go," she said as she grabbed his hand and hurried him away.

They walked in silence for a few blocks before he stopped her. "The lady in the elevator… Did she speak to you?" he asked.

Thinking it to be an odd question, she realized that the woman in the elevator must have been *the* other woman. Oh, how that woman had made her feel amazing… She realized that the same woman had made her husband feel the same way.

Damn well knowing that two wrongs do not make a right, she thought the better of it telling him what happened. "Yes, she did that… and more."

She said with a smile on her face as she reached out and pulled him into a kiss.

The ool

The door was heavy, it reminded her of the old castle doors in Croatia. Using both hands, she managed to open it with enough force that made a noise when it hit the wall. *Wow,* she thought. *Do not know my own strength.*

The room echoed with sounds of laughter and discussion. It took her a moment to adjust to the dim lighting of the bar. Looking around, she could not see anyone she knew, so she took the seat closest to the wall, where she could sit and be the watcher.

They met by accident. She was not supposed to be at the bar until later but decided that after the day, she needed a drink and some alone time. She saw him sitting at the bar, laughing with friends and flirting with some women sitting next to him. She saw him as a player—that smooth-talking guy who used his charm to lure prey into his trap. He would touch a woman's hand, rub his fingers along her arm, and then repeat the same action with the next one who caught his eye. She could hear his voice over the others and detected a slight accent. God, how she was turned on by certain accents.

On his way to the bathroom, he passed beside her and noticed the bracelet she was wearing. He had seen that necklace before but could not quite place it. Returning from the bathroom, he glanced over to see her. His eye kept looking at the bracelet on her arm. He was getting frustrated, as he always did when he could not remember something. Changing course, he walked over to her table.

"Excuse me, but where did you get that bracelet?" he asked.

"This old thing? Picked it up at a small gift shop in Casares a few years ago. Why do you ask?"

He could not answer her because he honestly did not know why he was asking her.

"Are you alright?" she asked. He seemed to look lost for a moment.

Looking at her, he smiled and walked away. Watching him walk away in silence, she wanted to laugh. But why would she laugh at him? She kept thinking of him as she played with the bracelet.

"Another drink?" the waitress asked. "Yes, and a menu please," she said as she realized that she had not eaten anything since breakfast. She was starting to feel the wine.

"Here you go. Oh, by the way, that guy that spoke with you a few moments ago? Don't bother with him," said the waitress as she picked up the empty wine glass and walked away.

This only made her more curious about who he was. She continued to watch him as he played his game with the women. He was the knight in a game of chess, moving to one woman then zigzagging to the next woman if he did not receive a response from the first. *Oh, these women, the pawns in his little game.* But she couldn't help but wonder: what was his end game?

He leaned between the two women he was talking to and looked around until he could see her. Still, she sat alone against the wall, just watching everyone. He could not understand how a woman so beautiful could be alone.

"What are you doing here?" he asked as he took a seat next to her. Placing her glass of wine down in front her, she rested her elbows on the table, held her chin, and smiled at him.

"Watching you," she said.

He was taken back by her response and started to laugh. "Are you enjoying what you see?"

Now there he was, blunt and smooth. She felt at a loss for words. It took her a moment to compose herself before answering him. "Well, you are handsome and, from what I have seen, a real charmer." She picked up her glass of wine to moisten her throat.

They sat in silence for a bit before he asked her, "What were you imagining as you watched me?"

"What you are like in bed. Are you very passive with your women or are you aggressive and controlling?" she asked.

He had to laugh at her bluntness but didn't know what to say until she asked, "How would you fuck that brunette you were chatting with? The one with big boobs hanging out of her top."

Looking over his shoulder, he knew how he would fuck her; it would be meaningless sex—no foreplay, just raw sex. "How do you think I would fuck her?" he asked her as he edged his way closer to her.

"You would be like a high school boy, just wanting to get your thrill so you could tell your buddies all about it. Probably would not last more than ten or fifteen minutes, tops" she said as she drank the last of her wine.

"You want to go somewhere quieter so we can talk and get to know each better?" he asked as he motioned for the waitress.

She went against everything in her being that told her not to go. "Sure," she said as she stood up and straightened her skirt.

The night air was warm, and the streets were bustling with people rushing to get somewhere. She wondered where he was going to take her and started to question her decision to go, but there was something about him that made her feel comfortable.

"Here we go," he said as he stopped in front of an old, dilapidated building. She could smell the faint scent of pot and urine. Entering the building, she was shocked to see such a beautiful interior. The room had walls of old brick and exposed wooden beams. In the center, there hung a massive chandelier with crystals that sent shadows across the room. Grabbing her hand, he walked her to a table that reminded her princess fairy tale picture books. There was an alcove in which a jazz band was playing; the band was made up of three men and a woman. They were all dressed as if they were playing in an underground 1920's club. The ambiance made her feel as if she had entered a time warp.

He was a connoisseur of red wine and chose a bottle of Pinot Noir that he knew she would enjoy.

"Impressive" she said. "Are you a sommelier?"

Laughing, he nodded his head. "No, put myself through school working summers at a winery in upstate New York. You learn a lot about wine after four years."

He confused her. The man in the bar, the man she had taken for a knight, was now the silent pawn moving his way through life.

"So, what do you do besides flirt with women in bars and bring them to out-of-the-way jazz clubs?"

He could not get over how naturally beautiful she was. He eyes were a shade of blue that he had never seen before. Her hair was golden with a hue of red that shone like the morning sun on a wheat field. "I am a wood pattern maker," he said.

"I'm sorry, you are a *what*?" she asked with a look of confusion on her face.

Laughing, he took her hand and placed it on top of the wood table they were sitting at. "Look here," he said as he started to show her the many patterns on the table. "I travel the world, mostly to logging villages where I find wood for clients that want specific pieces made for their homes. I look at what they want, lay out the wood I find, and construct the wood into sectional patterns that are eventually used to form sand moulds for castings or for a one-of-a-kind piece."

He continued to hold her hand as he waited for a reply. "Nope, never heard of it," she said. She smiled at him, wondering if he would kiss her before the night was over.

They listened to the band play before she asked him if he wanted to dance. They were playing Louis Armstrong's "It's a Wonderful World," a song she would dance to with her dad as a child. He accepted, and he held her close as they danced. She could feel his breath on her neck. Stopping in the middle of the song, he leaned in and kissed her. She could see the shadows of the crystals against his face, outlining his sculptured jaw and his deep, dark eyes. She knew that she wanted him.

She had always been a strong woman, the kind who never allowed a man to take control of her. She had always been the one in control; she decided where she would go. Nobody was to determine her destiny but herself. Yet here she was, in the middle of a room that resembled a Croatian castle with a knight who was kissing her and controlling her emotions.

Where am I? she started to wonder, but the thought faded as quick as it came.

"Let's go!" he said as he wrapped his arm around her waist and led her through a door that took them into yet another world.

He closed and locked the door behind them. She stood there, lost, not knowing where she was but feeling that she was where she needed to be.

"Come," he said as he held her hand and walked her toward an opal-shaped window that stood above the water.

She could smell the fresh sea air and hear the waves crashing below. Looking up, she saw the stars and the moon, and she believed that she had been transported to a new world. He held her close, and she could feel his heat his mouth now gently kissing the nape of her neck as he unbuttoned her blouse. She was mesmerized by his touch. She turned and gave him a kiss as she let her blouse fall. He stepped back, looking at her. Removing his shirt, he smiled.

"Let's play fair, now," he said.

"Play fair?" she asked.

"I am bare chested, so should you be too,"

Smiling, she removed her bra and stood there, watching him admire her. Not wanting to wait any longer, she dropped her skirt and walked to him. Her naked body with the moonlight amplified his desire for her. Grabbing at the waist of his pants, she pulled him forward and unbuckled his belt, slowly unzipping his pants as she looked deep into his eyes. His pants fell to the floor, and now it was her turn to step back and look at his naked body. She could feel the heat between her legs, her heart beating faster, and her nipples getting erect from the sea breeze.

"Take me," she said.

He reached out his hands and pulled her close, kissing her as he played with her nipples. She let out a slight cry. His hands slowly teased her as he played with her senses until he reached between her legs. Parting her legs, his fingertip slightly touched her throbbing clit. She bit his lip in anticipation of to the next thing he would do to arouse her.

"I want you," he said. "I want you, always."

Their bodies pressed together. Her nipples touched his chest, her thighs clamped his hips, and their faces embraced. Together, in harmony, they savoured each other. It was more than sex or a meeting of skin—it was an emotional bond that was bringing them together.

"I want you," he said.

With every inch of her being, she gave herself to him. "There. Yes, that's the spot," she said as her eyes widened, and her breathing intensified. There was moment of panic before her orgasm. "Yes," she said, "yes!" She reached her orgasm with him.

She rested against the window listening to the sounds of the waves as she made a wish on the brightest start she could see. Silently, she said, "Star bright, star bright, the brightest star in the sky tonight, I have a wish. I ask of you to please, oh *please* make it come true. I wish that he will stay with me."

Turning from the window, she saw him standing in the shadow, looking at her. "I can't keep my eyes off you," he said as he walked out of the shadows into the moonlight shining into the room. "Meet me here again tomorrow, downstairs at our table." Kissing her, he turned and left her there alone.

Walking into her apartment, she felt like she had just walked out of a dream. How could it have been real? How could she still feel his touch? How could she still want him?

"Who is he?" she asked aloud. She found it hard to sleep, for she wanted to know more about him and anticipated their meeting again tomorrow.

Eventually, she fell asleep. She did not need to dream, for she had just lived a dream. She woke up to her phone ringing.

"Hello," she said as she pushed herself up against the pillow.

"Good morning! Sleep well?" he asked.

She could feel herself smile. "Like a baby."

All she could think about was his smile and how looking into his deep, dark eyes made her feel like she was special. His touch made her feel something she had not felt in a long time. How could he make her feel like this?

Tantalizing Desires

"You know, I woke up this morning and the first thing I thought about was you. I needed to see you. I want to forget work, forget whatever today was supposed to be, and just see you. What have you done to me?" he asked with a laugh. "Will you meet me tonight?" he then asked.

"Definitely. I need to see you again," she said as she felt her cheeks flush.

She waited for him outside the jazz club. She was scared that he may not show. Checking her watch for the firth time, she felt a hand on hers. Turning, she saw him standing before her. His deep, dark eyes smiled as he leaned forward and kissed her. Grabbing her hand, he walked her through the door to the club.

"This way," he said as he led her to a corner of the room that had a small round table and two large wooden stools. The little corner was situated such that they could see everyone, but they were hidden enough that nobody could see them. The waitress approached with two glasses and some wine. The wine was in the kind of bottle that she had only seen in old movies set in the seventeenth century.

"This is a demijohn bottle," he said. "The wine is not as old as the bottle, but I thought it would be interesting considering the setting we are in."

All she could do was smile and think of how romantic he was. How did she get so lucky?

Leaning in, he kissed her. "Are you wearing underwear?" he asked.

She could feel herself blushing. After kissing him back, she said, "No."

Reaching under the table, he parted her legs with his warm hand. Slowly, his hand moved up her thigh. She could feel the sensation building between her legs. He reached her clit and started to tease it with his finger. She looked around to be sure nobody was watching them.

"Don't worry. We can see them, but they cannot see us," he said. Teasing her a little more, he brought her stool closer to him. "Spread your legs more. I have a surprise for you."

She did as he asked, wondering what the surprise would be. Just then, the waitress returned, pulling a curtain hidden on the side wall. The waitress approached her stool and introduced herself.

"Hello, I am Juliet. I will be your lady in waiting for the evening," she said as she kneeled her face inches from her throbbing pussy.

"Tell Juliet what you want her to do to please you. Anything you have fantasized about can now be real," he said.

Not knowing what to say but knowing that she was hot and extremely aroused, she told Juliet, "Lick my pussy till I ask for more." She could not believe that these words had come from her mouth.

Juliet began to lick her pussy. Her tongue lightly teased her clit, and then she slowly outlined her vagina with her warm tongue. Arching in her stool, she could feel his arm holding her so she would not topple backward.

"Tell her what else you desire," he whispered in her ear.

"Use your fingers to fuck me as you lick me," she said as her voice trembled.

God, it felt so good. She reached and grabbed his leg, sliding her hand up until she could feel his erect penis under his jeans. He undid his pants and guided her hand to his penis. She moaned as she felt his throbbing erection. She wanted him inside of her, but what Juliet was doing felt so good. Her body arched more, and she pushed herself forward to feel Juliet's fingers deeper inside of her. She could feel the orgasm building. Holding his penis in one hand, she grabbed

Juliet's head with the other, pushing her clit deeper into her mouth. Before she knew it, she was having an orgasm like never before.

Juliet raised herself, asking, "Anything else I can do for you?" Before she could answer, he raised her from the stool and directed her to lean on the table. Juliet took this as her cue to leave. Moments later, she could feel him taking her from behind. Holding her hips and pulling her as close to him as he could, he rapidly thrust into her, moving hard and fast. He pushed himself deep inside of her until he came. Together, they stood there catching their breath.

"Are you good?" he asked her as he stepped away and zipped up his pants. "Yes, never better," she said with a smile on her face.

Days turned into months, and months turned into a year. Their romance blossomed into a life of adventure. Their sexual exploits took them to realms of ecstasy that she had only ever fantasized about. They spent every moment they could together, except when he would travel for work. Even then, their phone sex was as powerful. She always hated to see him leave and would let him know that she would miss him.

"You should never feel the need to miss me," he would say.

But she did. She kissed him goodbye in the car—he never liked her to get out of the car when he knew he would be away for a long time. He found it hard not to cry as he let go of her.

The phone rang in the middle of the night, waking her.

"Hello?" she said in a groggy voice.

"It's me," he said. "Have you learned not to miss me yet?" he asked.

She thought it to be an odd question, and she asked him if he was alright.

He was surprised that he was able to form more than two words. "You need to not miss me because I need to stop missing you." he said.

She sat there lifeless, her heart beating in her stomach. Her head raced as she repeated the words she had just heard. Her normally poised and practical self had just disappeared. She tried to say something, anything, but she was lost in a whirlwind.

"It may just be for now, but it needs to be," he said.

Her words stumbled as they came out of her mouth. "I understand," she said as tears welded up in her eyes. She dropped the phone and fell to her knees. What would she do without him?

Steadying herself, she managed to get back on the bed. She licked the tears that reached her mouth and the salty taste remined her of their first night together. She could feel the emptiness filling her as her emotions started to build. Standing up again, she looked at herself in the mirror and asked herself, *How did you lose him?* She walked into the shower and let the warm water take over her as she cried.

That evening, she walked to the club—their spot, their getaway, their escape from reality. She pulled on the door and walked in to find the place empty. The massive chandelier? Gone. The princess wooden table? Gone. The round table with the massive stools? Gone. The jazz group? Gone.

"May I help you?" asked a woman dressed in a handsome suit.

"The club? What happened to the club?" she walked further into the empty building. Raising her voice, she asked again. "Where is everything?"

The woman walked toward her and held out her hand. "Come with me."

Taking her hand, she followed the woman into the room where she had first made love with him.

"The window is still there, as is the ocean. The rest is gone with him," she said.

He had played her so well that she never realized what had happened. A whirlwind romance that she believed would last forever was gone before she had the time to understand what had been done to her. She had seen the signs but chose to ignore them because she also saw other signs—the ones he wanted her to see. Or maybe she had just imagined them. She had convinced herself that he was different, that he meant everything that he said. She felt like a fool.

"I guess he had nothing to prove. He will be alone with nobody to love him or wait for him as I did," she tried to convince herself.

A few days later, she was contacted by his friend, Marc, asking if she was okay. Marc knew how much she loved him and could only wish that his friend would have the sense to come back to her. He knew they were meant to be. Even if this was true, he could see how much pain she was in.

Her family and friends told her "time heals all wounds," along with every other cliché known to humankind. But she knew him better than anyone, and deep down inside, she knew that he would be back for her picking up right where they left off.

Time passed and through it all, she never lost her smile. This led them all to believe that she was over him. Hiding her feelings was her forte. She moved on as she needed to, until she met Antonio—a man she saw sitting in the coffee shop she frequented. He reminded her a lot of *him*. He *was* not him, but she needed someone; it was time to feel the void in her life.

"You cannot have my heart, Antonio," she said as she dropped her dress on the floor and walked to him. "But you can have my body," she said as he picked her up and carried her to his bedroom.

The riter

I knew that he was gone. I felt this emptiness inside of me, a void that needed to be filled. I knew that he was never coming back and that the bond we once shared had been ripped away. I stood in the shower, naked, with the warm water running down my – . I was cupping my breasts with my wet soapy hands, imagining I was feeling his touch. My body was aching to feel his touch again, remembering how his fingertips ran up and down my body while his hot breath would whisper in my ear, "I need you; I want you."

He was a genius. He was so clever that he made himself my security. And I loved him for his cleverness, his quirks, and his love for me. Our relationship was built on a cracked foundation that became a solid platform over time; we thrived on it for decades, playing a pivotal role in regulating each other's wants and needs.

Sometimes I would look at him like I was looking at a stranger, wondering who he really was and what made my desire for him so strong.

He was an artist with a talent to catch every feeling in his work. His strokes would identify person hidden behind the outward appearance of the model he was painting. He always said he would paint me someday. He said, "I will find the real you the day I paint you."

We had spent afternoons sitting drinking margaritas on the deck overlooking the ocean. How we ended up here is still a mystery to me. One moment, we were in his tiny Soho apartment; the next moment, we were here.

I remembered it all so vividly. He looked so serene and romantic sitting in his Egyptian cotton harem pants, shirtless with beads of sweat trickling down his sun-painted chest. His brown eyes looked deep into my soul, teasing me with passionate desire to make love in the sand below. I sat there, bewitched by his chest, which heaved with desire to take me.

I have never desired a man as much as I desired him at that moment. My body was burning with lust and desire, but most of all it burned with love. I had never wanted to possess a man as much as I wanted to possess him.

I sipped my margarita, and then I reached over and touched his chest, teasing his nipples with my wet tongue. My hands slowly caressed his torso, reaching for the tip of his penis, which now stood hard and erect against his harem pants.

"I am going to freshen up. It's going to be a late night," he looked at me and smiled as he ran his fingertips softly up and down my arm, sending shivers between my legs. "I'll join you," he said, "Just give me a moment."

He entered the bathroom and saw my naked body behind the shower door. I was shadow in the steam waiting anxiously to be taken to levels of ecstasy where only he knew how to take me. Would this be the picture he would paint?

He opened the shower door and came in behind me. "You want me?" he asked as he traced his fingers along the nape of my neck and down my back until he reached my ass.

He gently cradled each cheek in his hands while he nibbled my neck. My body arched, and I ached to feel him. I placed my hands on the wall as my body tingled with desire. My knees became weak. He grabbed me and turned me to face him, pulling my body close to his.

"You're wet," I said.

His harem pants clung to his body, and his erect penis and lower torso were sharply outlined. It was my turn to grab his wet ass, and I grinded my body against his. Looking deep into his dark brown eyes, I realized how much I loved him.

This moment was like a dream. I prayed that I would not wake up. Our breaths got deeper and hotter. My pussy was beating against the feel of his penis. Somewhere during this time, he had managed to remove his pants, and I felt his throbbing penis between my legs.

"I need you," I said.

He smiled and lifted me onto his hard penis. I could feel the wet tip of his penis and yearned to feel him deep inside of me. I wanted his sweet come to fill me. Right when I wanted him most, he entered me. His arm held me close, and my legs wrapped securely around his body. My body screamed with desire. He pushed himself deeper and deeper into me and thrust until we came as one.

If I had known that one day he would be gone, I would have savoured the moment for even longer. The pain I feel now is nothing to the pain that will come later. The pain is still better than the emptiness of living without him.

I had to stop thinking and place myself in the moment. I needed to connect with what reality was and more, so I needed to connect with him.

"Touch me," he said. He placed my hands in his and softly kissed each finger as he gazed into my eyes. "Stop thinking. Concentrate on me."

I looked at him like I was looking at a piece of art. I took in his dark brown eyes, which looked at me like no man had ever looked at me. I wanted to wrap my fingers around the curls of his black hair, which was lined with silver streaks that only enhanced his beauty. I wanted this picture to last forever, like art in a museum, but I wanted it to be part of my private collection, for my eyes only.

"Seize the moment," he whispered in my ear. This I did. Slowly, I kissed him, caressing his face with my hands. His eyes looked closed, and I could tell he was savouring the moment too. "Yes, my love, seize the moment, seize the moment."

I knew that he would never forget this moment—every time he closed his eyes, he would see me. He would remember me and remember this moment.

His submissive stance changed as I lowered myself to his penis. His thumb gently slid across my lips until they parted, and he pushed his penis inside my mouth. He tasted of sweat, and it was so salty on my lips. He held my head in his hands and guided me as I licked and sucked until his moans told me that he was about to come.

He raises me to him, lifted me into his arms, and took me to his art studio, where he laid me on the paper-covered floor.

"I am going to paint you as I make love to you," he said.

He got a paintbrush and slowly traced the outline of my body, teasing me as he reached the sensitive spots between my legs. His smile aroused me more as he continued to trace my body with the paint brush.

"Edible paint," he said as he held up the jar for me to see. He dipped the brush into the jar and painted his tongue. Then, his tongue became the paintbrush. His tongue started on my breast, and he painted my nipples until they were erect. "I like that color on you," he said.

He proceeded to paint my stomach, teasing his canvas with his fingers as he descended to my waiting pussy. My body arched as he slid his painted tongue down to my throbbing clit. His tongue teased me as he licked and sucked until I give in to him. I screamed in excitement; he continued until I squirted on his painted tongue.

He glided his wet tongue up to my lips, painting my body with this mixture of edible paint and my juices. He smiled as he kissed me, telling me that he would miss me when he was gone. I nodded, refusing to release him from my arms. I needed to hold him tightly so I would remember this moment when he was gone. I knew that I would miss him, but I never believed that he would never come back to me.

I was on my way to his art show in another country, knowing that he never painted me to be seen by others. Knowing that nobody would know who I was.

"Excuse me, Miss, where am I taking you?" his voice had a strong accent that I could not identify. I wondered if he was as lost as I was here.

"To the museum please," At this moment, I was disconnected from reality; I could only feel our last time together, and I remembered it like it was yesterday.

The museum stood somewhat out of place, like a polar bear in the desert. I hesitated but knew that I had to go in. The steps seemed to go on forever. Step by step, my heart was beating. Was it fear or anxiety? I only knew that I needed to get through those doors.

I walked in, my heart beating so loudly that I could not hear myself think. I stood and looked around until I found the direction I needed to go. As I walked into the room, I could sense him—even smell him—but I knew he was gone.

"It's you," a voice said behind me. I turned to see an image of someone that I could not identify, as I was blinded by the image hanging on the wall.

"It's me," I said. "He painted me."

As I walked toward the image, the people parted, making a path for me. I could hear the faint whispers saying, "It's her! It's her!" I stood looking at the painting, wondering when he had painted this image of me. This image of me naked, lying in his bed, with curtains blowing in the wind. I could feel the sea breeze as if I were in the picture.

"I'm so happy you came. You know that I wanted you here." Gently he placed his hand on my lower back, sending a wave of heat through my body. Awkwardly, I turned and tried to say something, but the words would not escape my mouth. I thought that he was gone I had honestly thought that he was gone.

The last time I saw him was the day I ran down three flight of stairs barefoot, tears streaming down my face, knowing that I would never see him again. I remembered telling him that I would wait for him, and he smiled, kissed me, and said goodbye.

"What do you think?" he asked me. It was then that I realized that I no longer needed to go back in time. I was here with him now.

"Wow," was all I could say. He laughed, and his brown eyes lit up. I reached up and moved the curl from his brow. Smiling at him, I held his face in my hands and kissed him. I needed to know that this moment was real.

"I don't ever remember posing for this painting," I said. He brushed my cheek with his lips and slowly moved closer. He whispered in my ear, "I painted it from memory. Did I do you justice?"

Did he do me justice? He did more than that. He painted me such that all my dreams—my thoughts, my desires—were on display. I was uninhibited in his work. I felt a sense of freedom looking at it. I felt like an eagle flying and looking down at who I really was from above.

"Come," he said. "Let me introduce you to some people." He grabbed my hand and walked me over to a group of people. These were people from a world very removed from mine. These were artsy people who probably never worked a day in their lives.

"Sebastian, allow me to introduce you to my inspiration."

"Enchantée, Mademoiselle. He has never painted anything as beautiful as you."

An attractive woman joined our conversation. "Nonsense, she is much more beautiful than the panting. Allow me to introduce myself. I am Camelia. I have seen many of his pieces, and this one, my darling, is the most powerful one he has ever painted. I do not know what control you have over him, but he has brought out the best of himself through you."

I was introduced to many more people that evening, and I started to see his life outside of me. This life was so different from his life in the Soho Flat on McDougal Street. Who was this man? It did not matter who he was, because at this moment, everyone believed him to be mine and I was fine with this.

The evening slowly tapered down to a handful of people who wanted to celebrate his success.

"Is this your place?" I asked.

He looked at me and laughed. Then, he said, "Yes, this is my place. Come on, let us go."

We jumped into a waiting limo with the others and headed down a winding road covered in trees. You could see glimpse of water between the trees, and the moonlight guided us. Champagned added some more levity to the ride. Sitting next to him, I could feel his warmth. The heat from his body intensified the warmth I was feeling between my legs. My mind started to wonder to that place where only he could take me.

"Okay everyone, we have arrived."

I stepped out of the limo to see a quaint country cottage, which sat among paths of trees and shrubs lit up with fairy lights. At the entrance sat an ornate lion that seemed out of sorts.

"Everyone, welcome to my abode." As I stood outside the door looking into the night, he came up behind me and pulled me closer to him. I could feel his groin against my lower back and yearned to feel him deep inside of me. He kissed by neck and bit my ear.

"Come on in. You will have plenty of time to take all this in tomorrow."

The evening was a delight of small talk, champagne, and good food. Sebastian was a character with many adventure stories to tell.

"Oh, Sebastian, you must tell her the story of us," says Camelia.

"Us? You'll have to be more specific, for there are too many to tell of my love."

They both laughed and shared a passionate kiss before Camelia grabbed my hand and whisked me away. We entered a room that hosted a bed fit for a queen and a view of the night sky. The horizon went on forever, as if there was no end.

Camelia smiled and slowly caressed my back, she gently pulled on the straps of my dress and let it fall to the floor. I immediately covered myself, almost as if I felt shamed.

"Don't be so modest. You see, I had seen your nakedness before I even met you. You are like a vison that he has told me about, time and time again."

She walked around me, pulling my arms away from my breasts, and proceeded to play with the elastic of my panties. She slowly bent and pulled them down my legs. I could feel her warm breath, and then I felt her tongue as she guided her way back up. Her tongue reached my breast, flicking my nipple until it stood erect. She did it again, then she stepped back as if admiring her work.

"Turn around."

I slowly turned, feeling a warmth throughout my body. Her hands gripped my ass, fondling it in admiration.

"So tight, so firm." Gently her hands moved between my legs from behind, teasing me with her manicured fingertips. She slid a finger into my wet pussy, as if she were savouring every inch of me. I moved my legs apart, and she slid a second finger into me as she gripped my breast with her free hand.

I moan with pleasure, arching myself to feel her fingers deeper inside of me. She bit my neck as she pulled me closer, asking me if I wanted more. My moans told her that I did, and she slid yet another finger into me as I squirmed. She reached deep inside me until I came.

She removed herself from me and turned me around, placing her fingers in my mouth to make me taste myself.

"You're mine now, just as you are his," she said. Then she walked out of the room. I quickly gathered my dress and undies, got dressed and headed back out to the living room.

"Ah, there you are," he said. "Did you and Camelia have a good chat?" He winked then gave me a kiss. "You taste lovely," he said.

After everyone left, we headed to bed. As I crawled into bed next to my old love, I could tell he was about to fall asleep. I placed my hand on his limp penis and started to caress him.

"Wait," he said. "Just let me rest a bit. I just want to hold you close to me and savour this moment." He held me in his arms, and we feel asleep with the ocean breeze upon us.

In the morning, I waited next to him, not wanting to disturb him. As I looked out to the ocean, he rolled over and asked me what I was thinking about. I turned and looked into his deep, dark eyes. I saw my reflection.

"I thought you were gone. I thought I would never see you again. I thought you forgot me."

His eyes widened, his fingers traced the outlined of my face, and he kissed me. "I never forgot you."

My eyes watered he continued to kiss me. Between kisses, he said, "*Mi amor, has hecho un lugar en mi corazón y no quiero que ese lugar vuelva a estar vacío nunca más.*"

We made love, exploring each other's bodies as if it were the first time.

We spent the day exploring the grounds. "Have you taken in all the beauty that surrounds us?" he asked while holding me closely.

"I've taken in everything I can, yet as I look around, I can't seem to find the words to describe what I have seen."

As we headed back to the cottage, we saw a faint figure in the distance. Approaching the figure, I realized that it was Camelia. My body tingled with delight as I admired the curves outlined in her form-fitting dress. Her breasts were slightly exposed, and she wore a single pearl on a gold chain, which nicely sat in her cleavage.

"Ah, there you are," she said as she kissed his lips in an erotic fashion. She left a trace of her lipstick on his face; it glistened in the sunlight. Then she turned to me. "Well, my dear, you are looking more beautiful than when we last saw each other." She placed her hand in mine as we walk to the cottage.

Entering the cottage, Camelia shouted out, "Champagne!" as she placed a glass in our hands. "We are celebrating the best work our man has presented in quite some time. The fact that his muse has shown up only made it more successful. Cheers!"

As we sipped our drinks, she whispered into his ear. He smiled and said, "But of course I will."

As he looked at me, I smiled and asked, "You will what?"

"Camelia believes that my work can only be enhanced by my must being by my side to inspire me. I want you to stay here with me."

I was taken by his words, but before I could reply, Camelia drew me into her arms and kissed me. Her mouth parted, and her warm tongue was teasing me.

"Come," she said as she guided me to the same room she had brought me to the night before. She turned and looked at him, "Well? Are you not going to join us?"

He followed us, closing the door behind him. Camelia sat me on the edge of the bed as she proceeded to seduce my man. He complied with the simplicity of a child. Camelia ripped open his shirt, tracing the outline of his muscles with her manicured fingers and leaving red traces behind. Slowly, she unbuckled his pants. She glanced over her shoulder to be sure that I was watching. I wanted to tell her to stop, that he was mine, but her seductive approach only titillated me.

She removed his pants as he stood there like a statue, with his manhood exposed and erect. "Undress," she said, and I did. She sat him down next to me. Standing before us like a school matron about to punish us, she removed her dress and stepped closer to us. Grabbing my hand, she placed one on his hard-throbbing cock and the other between her legs. "He belongs to me, and I want you to make us both come."

I was mesmerized by it all. Parts of me wanted to say no, but other parts of me wanted to feel her control. I did as she asked of me, and I played with them both.

Later that evening, the three of us sat watching the sunset. As the stars started to appear, he grabbed my hand and asked me, "Will you stay here with me?"

I wanted to say, "Yes, I will stay with you forever." But I had to ask myself if I really wanted a life with him, knowing that Camelia owned him and that I would never truly be his. So, instead of following my heart, I looked deep into his loving eyes and said, "No."

His removed his hands from mine asking, "Why?"

I replied, "*Porque te amo tres mil.*"

As I stood up and started to walk away, Camelia asked, "Who are you?"

I replied, "*Yo sol la escritora.*"

The Goodbye

She had played the role of the fool long enough to know that it had to end. The hardest part was saying goodbye while there was still hope in her heart. She kept reading the signs that told her she was being the fool, but the memories kept her holding on. How many times would she replay his words over and over in her head, still believing that they were true? Her strength was running out, and she was preparing to run away. That way, if he did return, she would never see him at the coffee shop or the bistro down the street from where they lived.

They say you have three true loves in your life. Each love is for a different reason. Your first love is usually from high school or college. It's the love that you learned about from romantic movies or novels. Your second love is the one you must work hard on. This is the one where you learn what relationships are all about and what type of love you really want. Your third love is the one that catches you when you least expect it. It's the love that you think will not last because you have been hurt before, and you have stopped yourself from wanting to fall in love. Yet, this is the love that we make sacrifices for, the one that tells us why those we have loved before are not in our life anymore. This is real love.

Her first love was the boy down the street. They would stand and wait for the school bus together—him in his school uniform of blue shorts, a white shirt, a blazer, and a tie, and her with her white shirt, navy socks, and tunic. She also had her funky eyeglasses and a patch-covered eye. He though her to be a pirate and would ask, "Where might your parrot be?" She would kick or punch him. He would always sit next to her on the bus until they arrived at school. Then she would not see him until recess.

One autumn day during recess, he ran up to her and asked her to play a game with the others. They stood in a circle singing, and the boys in the inner circle walked around until the song stopped. Then, they would turn to the girl in front of them, hold her hand, and dance. She had hoped he would stop in front of her, and he did. Later that day on the bus ride home, he stayed on until it was her stop. He walked her to her front door and kissed her, but he ran once he saw her dad approach. She yelled at him, "Bye Brian," and walked into the house, completely in love.

By high school, she caught the eye of many guys, but her eye remained fixed on just one. She had not seen him since the fourth grade—his family had returned to Italy. Yet one day, there she saw him standing in the park with all his buddies. He caught a glimpse of her from the corner of his eye, and she walked toward him. Smiling, she gave him and hug and realized the last time they were together, he had kissed her and told her they would get married.

"Tony, remember me?" she asked. His cheeks turned red as he admired her beauty. There were no more messy curls hanging from the ponytail, no more socks pushed down to the ankles. Here she stood in ripped jeans and her hippy blouse, with her managed curls outlining her tanned face and her beautiful blue eyes.

Years later, she found her second love—the one who taught her what love was, how she wanted to be loved, and how she could love him. They married young—she was eighteen and he was twenty, but they managed school and work well. They followed a schedule, and it worked well for them. Work would separate them for periods of time, but they were comfortable with it because they had trust. She knew that he had a secret or two, but she also knew he loved her and would always protect her.

One say, an accident took it all away from her; his plane crashed, and she was suddenly alone.

As the years went by, she dated and remarried, but it was not a love marriage like she had before. She was comfortable with him and they enjoyed each other, but one day, they realized that she could not give him what he wanted. She could not give him all of herself. He left after a few conquests along the way.

She never expected to love again until she met the man who would become her third love. He made her feel comfortable. He said the things she needed and wanted to hear. She missed him when he was gone, even if was only for a few days. Her stomach filled with butterflies every time she read the words that he sent her. She understood who he was—or she thought she did—until he stopped being there. Yet, she still had hope even when he shut her out of his life.

As she cried in the shower, she asked herself, "Was I a fool to believe? Am I a fool to still have hope?"

She toweled herself dry, sat at the edge of the bed, and realized that she *was* a fool. She had to say goodbye, but she knew she would not. Having hope and believing gave her something. Facing reality meant that she would be alone. Better to have company in a fantasy that loneliness. This is what kept her going.

Her grandfather had once told her something that she held close to her heart. He had said, "Nobody can ever do you any good by loving you. You have all the love that you could ever want or need. But people could do you good by letting you love them, and that isn't easy."

She never knew what this meant until she found her first love. He loved her more than she believed anyone could love another. She loved him and knew that this was all the love she could ever want or need. When she lost him, she found herself in a world that was different from the one she used to know. Often, she would ask herself how she would get through the next day and the day after that. She got through them all, and with every day that passed, she grew to become stronger than she thought she could ever be. Her second love came along as an answer to what was missing in her life. She believed that she loved him, but she knew she was not in love with him. He was the person to fill the void that missing.

Her second love was, as they said, "the one you need to work on," but she could only work as hard as her heart would let her. He left her to raise two children on her own. She gave up parts of her life to ensure that they had what they needed to grow into the strong people that they are today. Her second love held her prisoner after he left. Her heart was locked away, not wanting to be given to anyone. She felt that she had to give what little love she had to her children. So, she held herself prisoner to the children she loved, and she tried to prove to the man who left her that she was still that strong woman.

Before her third love, she had chosen not to let anyone else into her life. Yet he walked into her life and, in no time, into her heart. She had been shocked that she let him in, but she trusted him and wanted him to have her heart. He was the first man in a long time that was letting her love again.

She thought that the fun they had together would make things easy. They were like two lost souls who finally found each other again. But this was not the case. Obstacles that got in their way, but they overcame them. Distance took them away from each other, but he knew that she was waiting for him.

Then, one day, she learned the truth. He did not need her in his life. She lost love for the third time.

Her stomach churned every time she thought of the words he wrote her, letting her know that he did not need her. Although the words may have said, "For now," she knew that in reality, "now" meant "forever."

She held on, thinking of conversations they had before he sent her that message. She would reinterpret his words and replace his meaning with her own. Hope was all she had. She knew that it may be a fantasy, a dream, a wish, or just hope that she would feel his arms around her again, but she also knew that for now, she needs the thought of him to feel safe.

When as other opportunities for love came up, she turned them down. The thought of sharing coffee and chit chat with another man made her feel like she would be cheating on him, even though she has no idea whether he had moved on. She had convinced herself that he would have told her if there was another woman, She continued to live in uncertainty because she did not want to believe that her third love was the last, that it had left her alone. Just the thought of being alone brought tears to her eyes.

I believe there should be a fourth love in our lives: The one where we hold control. In our fourth love, we decide where the path leads. We make sure the truth is heard and not hidden in a message of deceit. We have the foresight to know what lies ahead, and we can avoid the hurt.

Human closeness to someone with whom you are connected emotionally and physically should not be thrown away like garbage—it should be spread out on the floor, like pictures in a collage, and examined. I want to examine why I feel so hurt and unable to let go of my third love, especially when I feel that hope may be fading. I want that fourth love so that I can be in control and not be hurt again.

Now, to write my final letter.

The nterviews

People are lucky if they can say that they have fallen in love. Some fall in love more than once in their lifetime. Love does not know age or time. Some people say that they have fallen in love at first sight, others say that it has taken time. With love comes hurt. There is never an age, or a time limit attached to hurt. Everyone deals with hurt differently. Some cry, some talk about it to their friends, some say nothing and get through it on their own, and some find a reason to stay in love even when the person they love no longer loves them.

We had our hearts broken in high school and think that we can never survive the hurt, but we did. Then come the twenties, when we are questioning our being, our sexuality, our desire, our need to be wanted and loved. By thirty, we think we can have it all figured out—and you know, we probably do in some strange way. Forty hits and we question if we have missed anything in life. When we realize that maybe we have, then we ask ourselves if it too late.

As I wrote this book, I interviewed many people. I spoke with people I knew and learned more about them than I ever knew before. I spoke with people who were referred to me because they were swingers. Having spoken to these people about love, sex, and fantasies, I did learn quite a bit about myself and the things I want to try. Someone told me that in their forties, they re-explored a fantasy they first tried in their twenties. It felt different and familiar at the same time. Honestly, they could not explain what it meant to them.

Now, some people cannot distinguish between sex, fantasy, and love. Some combined them all together, which may make things complicated. I asked a few people to explain the difference between sex, love, and fantasy, just to get an overall idea of their perception of how these concepts intertwine.

Male #1, age 32

"Love is sex when you really care about the person and a fantasy is roleplay to keep things fresh."

Female #1, age 24

"Love is an emotion; sex is physical, and fantasy is just a game."

Male #2, age 22

"Sex is just fucking, love is having good sex and doing things that you would not do to a girl that you fuck, and fantasy is what you think of to get hard."

Female #2, age 34

"Love is a bond between two people, sex is making that bond between the two of you tighter, and fantasy is when you start getting bored with each other and need to spice things up."

Male #3, age 66

"Love is a deep devotion to a person that you want to spend your life with, sex is a beautiful act shared by two people that bring you as close as you ever can be, and fantasy is what I call fun you can have with no boundaries."

Female #3, age 52

"Love is trusting that the person you are with is always there for you to care for you like you care for them. Sex is something that keeps you together, something that only the two of you can share together. Fantasy is what makes the sex even better."

<u>Male #4, age 50</u>

"Love is knowing that you can share everything about you with someone. Your likes, dislikes, fears, and silly things. Sex is a release of your energy that you keep deep inside of you, and fantasy is what you wish you could have."

Like (noticeable respect), Love (deep affection), Admire (regard with wonder), Respect (proper acceptance): These are synonyms that identify our relationship with our partners. They all share the same connotation—some may sound a little more profound, but they are nonetheless the same. Sex (womanhood, manhood), Love (deep affection), Fantasy (vision, imaginative).

The fantasies I wrote are based on like, love, admire and respect. They are all fabrications of someone's imagination. But is a fantasy not just a characteristic of philosophical existentialism?

Either way, I know that everyone can relate to these fantasies because we are humans with feelings, needs, and desires. Place yourself into the role of the main characters. The male and female with whom you can relate. The nameless characters created so you can insert your own name in their place. I am allowing you to be the fantasy. I know that if you look hard enough, you will realize that you are the character with no name. Let these be your fantasies, and maybe they can come true.

I hope you enjoyed!

The Next Chapter

We are never sure how our fantasies are going to end. It all depends on you and what you decide. Nobody can tell you that your fantasy will never come true. It is your choice to make it come true or not.

I often was the one who was undecided knowing that time was not on my side. "Give me till the end of the month, I still have things that I need to figure out". They all knew that the outcome would be the same. The seed had been planted and it was up to me to decide if I would stay and see it grow or cut it down before it could bloom.

She hated how at the last moment my fantasy would be taken from me and never knowing for how long. Nobody ever told me anything as they felt the less, I knew the better it was for them. My opinion about them was averse to say the least, I had the intel on how they worked and made a promise that one day I would infiltrate them to have him back with me to make all the fantasy's a reality.

The company has been in business for less than 5 years making a name for themselves by taking on new projects that required people with specific skills. Most of the projects included building new industry using natural resources that were available to them. They needed him for his background in sustainable development. He had those skills after having worked overseas for other companies like this one building new cities that the company could profit from.

The company caused tension in our relationship. Most of which he brought on himself by not being honest with them leading them to believe that he had nobody waiting for him at him. The offers made to him were very alluring taking him away from me. If only he could be truthful and tell them that I was always here waiting for him, then maybe they could have asked him to bring me with him.

He always told me that it was his decision to go but I knew that they had the carrot dangling in front of him and he would follow if they promised him what he wanted. I always did question if he knew what he really wanted. I often questioned if he really wanted me to wait.

He started with them when they were new and grew with them as they became one of the most prosperous companies in the universe, so they claimed. He rose in rank with every mission he took only to come back and start over again. Did he not see this? Did he not understand their manipulative ways? Was he just another pawn for me to have to reprogram to be the man that I and every other woman longed for? When would it end? How could I stop it for the last time?

I looked across from my seat to see him sitting there, and this time it was really him not the imagine the company wanted me to see. They tried planting the seed with this one, but he was too stubborn to let them get close enough to him. The strategic thinker who refused to ever surrender. Handshake, pat on the back, drink? Nothing they tried could entice him. Now I was his to mold into the man all woman wanted.

My heart felt heavy, unsure if I could do what was asked of me. I knew if I molded him into the man, they asked he would never be who I knew him to be. I thought to take him away from all of this, but would he go? Am I strong enough to lose him if they took him first?

There were so many questions for him. Just me wanting to know how someone could turn so cold. How could somebody wake up one day and decide that they would feel no more. Why was is so impossible for his words to be spoken now that he realized they would plant the seed in him. How long before he could find the courage to tell them that he never wanted to hurt anyone, but he did, and he was okay with it.

I felt like the fool questioning myself as to why I let myself fall in love with someone who was like a machine, a robot, no emotion, no remorse unable to love. I knew that all love ever did for me had hurt me. All I ever asked for was to be loved and this I could never find because everyone I ever loved had left. No closure, no reason, just gone.

I knew that it was best for me to walk out into the depths of the unknown where nobody could hurt me. Lost amongst the souls. This would be better than planting the seed. This would be painless.

To be continued.

Lightning Source UK Ltd.
Milton Keynes UK
UKHW011545230921
391075UK00001B/332